I'm Glad He's Dead

Also from EATMS Productions

Books on power, survival, women's autonomy, and the systems shaping modern America.

Nonfiction

Billionaires, Capitalism, and Power

Evil and the Mountain Ungreed
Self Help for American Billionaires
Selfish Steve and the Ivory Tower
Tariffs, Taxes, & Face-Eating Leopards
Ban Billionaires: Fascism Fix

Fascism, Religion, and Cultural Control

Self Help for the Manosphere
Fascism 2025
Fascism & the Perverts & the Greed Virus
Christian Fascism Marriage Book
Tyranny, Table Manners, & Tiramisu

Guides for Women's Autonomy and Protection

How to Survive in Post-America as a Woman
Project 2025 American Drag
4B – Burn, Ban, Boycott, Build
4B OG – So No Go GYN
I'm Glad He's Dead

Analysis of Authoritarian Project 2025

Project 2025: The Blueprint
Project 2025: The List
Project 2025, Christian Dumb Dumbs, & The Republican Agenda
Fascism, Project 2025, & The Pinkprint

Modern Rewrites for Women

Stoic Principles Reimagined
Siddhartha Reimagined
The Prince Reimagined for Women
The Art of War Reimagined for Women
The Jungle Reimagined
The Constitution Reimagined for Women

Machine Learning Series

AI, Bitcoin, Nostr for Women
AI, Safety, & Security for Women
AI, Anxiety, & Health for Women
AI, Kids, & Family Safety for Women
AI, Creativity, & Personal Expression for Women
AI, Independent Work, & Parallel Power for Women

Social Systems Series

Emotional Labor for Women
Household Power for Women
Workplace Power for Women
Medical Bias for Women
Aging Systems for Women
Recovery Systems for Women

Fiction

Dystopian Stories of Resistance and Collapse

Propaganda Paige & the Missing Prosperity
Propaganda Paige & the TIDE Manifesto
Propaganda Paige & the Shadow Cartographers
Propaganda Paige & the Prosperity Alliance
Propaganda Paige & the Shattered Truth
Propaganda Paige & the Rising TIDE
Propaganda Paige & the Last Bastion
Propaganda Paige & the Dawn of Prosperity
Project 2025: Dorian — The Last Men
Project 2025: Boy — A Last Men Novel

I'm Glad He's Dead: Fascism Hurts

Empathy Island 2

by
Eloise Yarvin

Introduction by Esme Mees

EATMS
PRODUCTIONS

ISBN: 978-1-966014-32-4

Cover, interior design, interior prints by: Esme Mees

eatms@pm.me
www.eatms.me

Printed in the United States of America.

We can do this the easy way,
Or, we can do this the hard way.

— *stock phrase/trope*

Table of Contents

Introduction

This is what happens when you let men with power write the rules. We told you this was going to happen.

They call it security, but it's bombs in living rooms. They call it discipline, but it's a pastor sneering until a girl cuts her skin. They call it justice, but it's a badge and a gun pointed at a child's chest. They call it healthcare, but it's a scalpel used to silence a woman in pain. They call it acceptable losses. We told you this was going to happen.

This is what happens when the country turns into a stage where lies wear the costume of truth and the audience is told to clap or be dragged out. We told you this was going to happen. And this is what happens after.

The dead don't speak, but the living do. One by one, they come into the room. They sit under the weak light and answer the only question that matters. "Who are you glad is dead?" It is not pretty. It is not clean. But it is the truth. And, we told you this was going to happen.

Esme Mees, Fall 2025

~1
The Chamber Opens

The basement smelled like bleach and smoke, the kind of
mix that burns the back of your throat and makes your eyes
water before you realize why. The walls were bare concrete
and damp in the corners. Someone had dragged down
folding chairs from a church hall, those metal ones that
clatter if you breathe too hard. A single bulb hung from a
cord above the table, swaying whenever the furnace kicked.
Its light was thin, yellow, and nervous, like it didn't want the
job.

I sat in the metal chair with my hands folded on the table,
voice sweet as a candy wrapper.

"Oh gee," I said. "I'm glad he's dead."

Across from me, the boy flinched. He was maybe sixteen. His
hair was singed at the edges, his sweatshirt torn down the
sleeve. Soot smeared his face, but his eyes were clear, blue
like winter mornings before the frost melts. He sat hunched,
as if the ceiling might collapse again any minute.

He stared at me. "Who?" His voice cracked like the
lightbulb.

"The one who did this to you. The one who ordered it."

He hesitated. His lips parted and closed, and for a second I thought he might run. But then he leaned forward and whispered, "Yeah. Him."

"Tell me," I said softly. "What happened."

The boy gripped the edge of the chair as though it might bolt out from under him. "It was night. Late. I was playing a game on my console, half-asleep. My mom was on the couch, TV humming. My sister was in her room writing, she liked to stay up late, writing. Then everything went black. The power just cut. And before I could even breathe—" His voice broke. He swallowed and started again. "The whole place lifted. Like the ground wanted to spit us out. I heard this sound. Not thunder. Not a plane. It was like metal tearing the sky in half."

"What did you see when you came to?" I asked.

He blinked. "Red. Just red. My room didn't have walls anymore. My neighbor's car was sitting where the kitchen used to be. The fridge was torn open, milk steaming on the floor. I remember the smell, it was sweet, like sugar burning, mixed with gas and hair." His hands shook. "I saw my mom. Or, what was left. She'd been on the couch. The couch was shredded, springs sticking out like claws. She was gone. My sister—" He stopped. His lips pressed white.

"Say it," I told him.

He lifted his eyes to mine. "She was under the window. The blast threw her there. Her arms were glass. Shards all the way in, like stars. She wasn't moving. I thought maybe she was asleep."

The bulb flickered. The room smelled hotter, though nothing burned here.

12

"Who pressed the button?" I asked.

"The smug man. The one they send to the press room. The one with the maps and the circles and the fake smile. He said it was surgical. Clean. He said if there were casualties, they were acceptable."

"And your family," I asked, tilting my head, "were they acceptable?"

He gave me a look so sharp I almost admired it. "My mom cleaned houses but wanted to be a baker. My sister was fourteen. I was trying to beat a boss fight. The only thing dangerous in our place was the stove that never lit right."

I tapped the table lightly. "So why are you glad he's dead?"

"Because if he were alive, he'd keep calling people like us 'acceptable.' He'd keep pressing buttons like they were toys."

"Does his death make you whole?"

His shoulders slumped. "No. I still feel like I am choking. I still hear the whistle. I still taste pennies in my mouth. Whole rooms are gone from me."

"Then why glad?"

He slammed his fists on the table. The recorder I'd set there rattled and nearly tipped. "Because at least he can't do it again. Because the next kid might keep his mom. Because someone had to pay."

I let the silence stretch. The boy's breath sawed in and out, ragged and hot.

"And what about justice?" I asked finally. "Do you call this justice?"

He shook his head. "Justice would be them admitting what they did. Naming my mother. Naming my sister. Looking me in the eye and saying the words. Justice would be a grave with her name spelled right. This—" He clenched his fists again. "This is just the bleeding stopped for once."

The bulb above us swung, shadow slicing across his face like a blade. He kept talking.

"They said on TV we were a target. They said the strike was necessary. They said our house was hiding something."

"And was it?" I pressed.

He looked at me like I was stupid. "It was hiding my mom's bread in the oven. That's it. She was baking. It burned when the walls came down. That's all."

"Did anyone believe you?"

"No." His voice went flat. "The neighbors said the government wouldn't hit us without a reason. They said maybe my mom was mixed up in something. They said maybe my sister was talking to the wrong people online." His jaw trembled. "They said lies until I almost believed them myself."

I leaned closer. "And now? Do you still believe them?"

He stared at the table. "No. Maps lie when money draws them. Cameras lie when they only show what the wankers, I mean, bankers want. But my eyes, my eyes saw my mother. My eyes saw my sister. And my eyes aren't lying."

The silence after that was heavy. The room seemed smaller, the air thick. The boy's knuckles were raw where he'd scraped them on brick.

"What did you carry out?" I asked.

He blinked. "From the rubble. What did you carry?"

He opened his mouth, closed it, then said: "A piece of the door. Just a slab of wood, scorched. I dragged it out and sat behind it while the soldiers came. I talked to them through the hole where the knob used to be."

"What did they ask you?"

"If I was a combatant. If I knew any. If I could point to where they were hiding."

"And what did you say?"

He let out a bitter laugh. "I said the only thing hiding in my house was bread in the oven."

The bulb hissed. His shadow stretched across the wall, long and broken.

"Tell me one true thing about your mother?" I said.

His face softened. "She whistled when she cooked onions. Said onions hated being cut if you frowned. But if you whistled, they forgave you and wouldn't make you cry."

"That is her truth," I said. "And now it lives here."

He nodded once. His hands unclenched.

"And you," I asked, tilting my chin, "are you glad he's dead?"

"Yes." His voice didn't waver this time. "I am."

"Why?"

"Because he can't press another button. Because no more families have to hear that whistle and see their house come apart."

"Will that bring your family back?"

"No." His shoulders sagged. "But at least I'm not waiting for it to happen again."

I stood and clicked off the recorder. The bulb swung above us, creaking, as if the whole ceiling leaned closer to listen. The boy stared at the table, but his breathing had steadied. For the first time since he came in, his hands weren't clenched.

"Go," I said gently. "You've said what needed saying."

He rose, stiff and uncertain. For a moment, he looked like a man, too old for his age. Then the metal chair scraped behind him, and he was just a boy again.

He paused at the door. "Why are you asking me all this?"

"Because the world out there will try to bury it. And someone has to remember."

He nodded once, then pushed open the door. It groaned and closed with a thud. His footsteps faded up the stairs.

The basement went quiet again. Just the hum of the bulb and the faint tick of pipes in the walls.

I leaned back in my chair, crossed my legs, and let the silence thicken. My lips curled into a smile I'd practiced for years, sweet and sharp.

"Next," I said.

The basement didn't change much when the door closed behind the boy. Same swinging light. Same scorched smell clinging to the walls. But silence has a way of rearranging a room. After his story, the air felt heavier, like the weight of the whole house above was pressing down, daring me to keep going.

I stayed seated. Crossed one leg over the other. Smoothed my skirt like I was back onstage. "Oh gee," I said to the empty air, "I'm glad he's dead."

The hinges groaned again. Another figure slipped in. A girl this time, maybe seventeen, maybe younger if you scrubbed the grief out of her face. She wore a hoodie too big for her, sleeves chewed at the ends. Her hair hung damp across her cheeks. She avoided the light like it might interrogate her before I could.

"Sit," I told her.

She pulled the chair closer to the table, dragging the metal legs across the floor. That screech filled the room like a warning. She dropped into the seat and hunched low, both hands shoved into her sleeves.

"What's your name?" I asked.

She shook her head. "Doesn't matter."

"It matters here."

Her lips twitched. "Call me—" She swallowed. "Call me Rose."

"All right, Rose. Who do you say is dead?"

Her fingers gripped her sleeves tight. "Him."

"Which him?"

"The one who laughed."

"Tell me."

She took a long breath through her nose, then let it out in one sharp burst. "I told him no. He didn't care. He said no one would believe me. He said he could do what he wanted, because I was nothing and he was everything." Her voice cracked. She yanked her sleeve to her mouth, biting it.

"What happened?" My tone stayed steady, sweet but firm.

She shook her head, trembling. "Do I have to say it?"

"You don't have to say every detail," I said. "But you have to name the truth."

Her eyes flicked up at me. They were dark, furious. "He raped me. He pinned me down and laughed when I cried. And then he left me there, like trash on the floor."

The bulb buzzed louder. The room felt hotter, though the air was cold.

"And now?" I asked.

She sat very still. "He's gone. Someone told me he's gone."

"And are you glad?"

Her lips tightened. She nodded once.

"Say it."

"I'm glad he's dead."

"Why?"

"Because he can't do it again." Her hands trembled harder. "Because he can't grin in my face and tell me I don't matter. Because he can't make another girl feel like she's nothing."

"Does his death take back what happened?"

She shook her head violently. "No. Nothing takes it back."

"Does his death heal you?"

"No," she whispered. "I still smell him sometimes, even when I shower. I still hear him in the dark."

"Then why glad?"

Her voice sharpened. "Because it's over for him. Not for me, but for him. And that's something."

The silence after those words was sharp enough to cut skin.

I leaned closer across the table. "Tell me, Rose. What did you carry out of that night?"

Her eyes darted. She blinked fast. Then: "A bruise. Dark as ink. I pressed it every day for a week, just to feel something that was mine, even if it hurt."

"And now?"

"It faded," she said. "But I remember. I'll always remember."

"Do you want revenge?"

She hesitated. "I wanted it. I wanted him to know what it felt like. To choke. To beg. But he's gone. So all I have left is the gladness."

"Is gladness enough?"

Her jaw worked. "It's the only thing that's mine. They tried to take everything else."

I nodded. "Then we'll set it here, on the table. Gladness as your proof."

Her breathing slowed. She shifted back in the chair, as if setting it down made her a little lighter.

"And one true thing about yourself?" I said. "Not about him. About you."

She stared at me like she didn't understand.

"Something no one can erase."

Her lips parted. "I draw. My sister says I can make people look alive on paper. Like they're breathing, even when they're not there."

I smiled, but it wasn't a soft smile. "Then that is your truth. You draw, and the paper listens."

Her shoulders shook once, like a laugh she couldn't finish. She wiped her sleeve across her face.

"Do you hate him?" I asked.

"Yes."

"Will you always?"

She thought about it. "Maybe not. But I'll never forgive him."

"That is yours to decide," I said. "Hate, forgiveness, gladness, they all sit in your hands now."

The bulb above us buzzed and swung. Her shadow stretched along the wall, bent but unbroken.

She stood abruptly, chair legs screeching again. She looked at me, eyes sharp. "You going to ask someone else next?"

"Yes," I said.

"Good. Don't stop." She yanked the hood over her head and walked to the door.

I called after her. "Rose."

She paused.

"You said you make people look alive on paper. Make her alive too. Your sister. The one who told you that."

Her shoulders shook again, but this time it sounded more like a laugh. Then she pulled the door open and slipped out.

The room went quiet. The bulb hummed. The folding chairs sat like witnesses who couldn't speak.

I leaned back, crossed my legs, and let my lashes drop in a wink no one saw.

"Next," I said.

~2
The Paper Chains

The basement had not changed. Same bare walls. Same chair waiting in the circle of light. The bulb buzzed above like an insect trapped in glass. The air was sour, heavy with old bleach.

I crossed my legs and leaned on the table. My voice came out steady, sweet, almost sing-song.

"Oh gee," I said. "I'm glad he is dead."

The door opened. A young woman stepped in. She carried herself like someone who had learned to walk carefully. Her backpack straps were still cutting lines into her shoulders, though the bag was gone. Her hair was tied in a knot that sagged as if it had been pulled too tight too many times.

She sat down without being asked. The chair squealed on the concrete floor. She set her hands on the table, palms flat.

"What is your name?" I asked.

"Call me Ana."

"All right, Ana. Who is dead?"

Her throat moved. "The low IQ man. The one who signed the paper."

"Which paper?"

Her eyes flicked up toward the bulb, then back to me. "The one that told me where I could go and where I could not. The one that told me what I could do with my body. The one that decided I was not mine anymore."

"Tell me what happened?"

She took a slow breath. "I was in college. First year. First taste of freedom. I had a car, a job at the bookstore, a boyfriend who made me laugh. I thought the world was wide open. Then the law passed. He stood in front of cameras and said it was for the good of the nation. He said girls like me needed guardrails, or we would lose ourselves. And then he signed, and made stealing my freedom the law of the land."

"What changed for you?"

"At first it was small. Extra ID checks at the dorm. Curfews. They said it was for our safety. Then it was bigger. Travel permits. If I wanted to visit home, I had to file forms weeks in advance. If I wanted to cross state lines, I needed permission. I was nineteen years old, and the low IQ man decided I needed a parent again."

"And your body?" I asked.

Her face twisted. "The paper said I could not make choices about it. They called it protection of life. They meant control. Suddenly doctors were afraid to treat me. I bled for three weeks once, and the clinic sent me home with Tylenol. They said the law tied their hands. I watched my own blood fill pads like water in a leaking boat. I thought I might die.

24

All because a man with a pen thought my life belonged to him."

The bulb above hummed louder, as though the room itself wanted to listen closer.

"Did anyone resist?"

She laughed once, sharp. "We marched. We held signs. We shouted outside his office until our throats were raw. He called us hysterical. He said we did not understand. He said he knew better than we did what freedom meant. Then he doubled down. He signed more papers. Each one tighter than the last."

"What did those papers feel like to you?"

She looked down at her hands. Her palms pressed harder into the table until they shook. "Chains. Thin as notebook paper, strong as iron. They wrapped around my wrists, my legs, my stomach. I could feel them even in my sleep. When I tried to breathe, the words on the page cinched tighter."

"Why did people obey?"

"Fear," she said quickly. "Shame. They said if you broke the law, you would ruin your family. They said you would be branded, marked, blacklisted. They said you would never work again, never marry, never belong. And some believed them. Others just got tired. It was easier to fold yourself small than to fight."

"And you?"

She met my eyes. "I folded for a while. I wore the right clothes. I lowered my head. I smiled when they checked my bag, even when it was empty. I swallowed my anger until it made me sick."

"Why?"

"Because I thought maybe I was wrong. That is how it works. They tell you enough times that you are reckless, sinful, irresponsible. You start to wonder if maybe you are."

"And when did that change?"

She sat straighter. "The day I buried my roommate. She was twenty. She wanted to finish school before she had a child. She tried to take care of it herself. She bled out in our bathroom. I held her hand until it went cold. The low IQ man never said her name. He called it another tragedy of irresponsible youth. That was when I stopped folding. That was when I stood up again."

The basement seemed to draw tighter around us. The bulb swayed slightly, shadows jumping across the walls.

"Tell me, Ana," I said. "Why are you glad he is dead?"

Her answer came without hesitation. "Because he cannot write chains anymore. Because he cannot sit behind a desk and pretend his pen is holy. Because every page he signed is now dust with him."

"Does his death give you back your freedom?"

"No." She shook her head. "I am still watched. I am still afraid. I still carry the weight of every rule he wrote. The chains do not fall away just because his hand rots in the ground."

"Then why glad?"

"Because at least no more chains will be written by him. He, being gone is one less low IQ man controlling us because they are pussies. Because now, he cannot press down on anyone else. Because the machine lost one of its gears."

"Do you think another low IQ man will take his place?"

"Yes. They always do."

"Then why celebrate his death?"

"Because he does not get to win forever. Because even if another takes his place, for one moment, he is gone. And I am still here."

Her voice cracked, but her eyes stayed hard.

"What did you carry out from that time?" I asked.

She thought for a long moment. "A page. One of the laws. I stole it from the courthouse during a protest. I keep it folded in my pocket. I spit on it sometimes. I burn its corner with a match and watch the words curl."

"And one true thing about yourself?"

She smiled faintly, a tired smile. "I run. Not away. For myself. I run until my lungs ache and my legs give out. And when I run, no one can catch me. That is mine."

I nodded. "That is your truth. You run, and no one catches you."

Her hands finally left the table. She leaned back, her shoulders lighter.

"Do you hate him?"

"Yes."

"Will you always?"

She closed her eyes. "No. One day he will just be bones. Then I will forget his name. But today, I hate him."

The bulb flickered and steadied.

She stood and pulled her straps back onto her shoulders, though her bag was gone. She looked at me one last time.

"You going to keep asking?"

"Yes."

"Good." She walked to the door.

Her footsteps faded up the stairs. The basement sighed back into silence.

I leaned back, folded my hands, and smiled that sugar-sweet smile again.

"Next," I said.

The bulb hummed like a trapped fly against glass. I clicked the recorder back on and set it near the edge of the table so it could hear everything. The basement smelled of bleach fighting a losing battle. I folded my hands and let the sugar drip into my voice.

"Oh gee," I said. "I'm glad he's dead."

The door opened on its groaning hinges. The figure at the threshold hesitated, then stepped in. They wore a denim jacket with a college logo peeling at the back. Their hair was chopped close with kitchen scissors, uneven and blunt. A campus badge swung on a lanyard against their chest, the plastic sleeve long gone.

"Sit," I said.

They pulled the chair into the circle of light, but pushed it back an inch so the glare would not fall directly into their eyes. Their hands were chapped. Their jaw was tight with the kind of anger that hardens after tears are gone.

"What is your name?" I asked.

"Call me Jules."

"All right, Jules. Who is dead?"

"The low IQ man," they said. "The one who liked to hold up the bill with his name across the top."

"Which bill?"

"The one that made my body a public project. The one that told my doctor what to deny me. The one that turned my campus into a checkpoint."

"Tell me what happened?"

Jules looked at the recorder, then at me. "I started school hopeful. I had a roommate who kept quiet, a job at the library, and a doctor who saw me every month to keep me steady. Then the bill passed. They made a ceremony out of it. The low IQ man stood with the governor and a row of men with smiles like cuts. They said they were saving children. They said they were protecting women. They never said my name. So I learned what their silence meant."

"What changed for you?"

"They shut my clinic. My doctor called me crying. She said she couldn't write me another prescription. She said the state would take her license if she did. She told me maybe I should move." Jules gave a sharp laugh. "As if my family had the money for that. The next month the pharmacy shrugged. The month after that my hands shook so bad in class I couldn't write."

"What happened on campus?"

"They set up a desk in the student center. Security. You had to show your ID to use the bathroom. If your face didn't match the box they expected, they sent you down the hall to an office. A woman with a cross on her neck explained the new policy with a soft voice and a hard smile. Housing rules changed. They said it was about protecting comfort. Comfort meant erasing people like me. One day a boy followed me from the dining hall and told me I was the reason his sister couldn't compete in sports anymore. He wanted me to apologize for existing."

"Did you?"

"No."

"Why not?"

"Because my existence is not a policy. It's me."

"And the law that declared you a terrorist threat?"

"Fear and more fear came. For me but mostly them, so scared are they. Those people have never really had to be afraid. So they take their weakness and they metastasize it. Then they send it out like a hound dog. A four legged-

pervert. That hound, it crawled in and sat on my bed. It followed me to the shower and stared through the curtain. It buzzed in my phone and told me where I could go. It turned my roommate into a mirror that only reflected what the low IQ man wanted to see."

"Why did people obey?"

"Because the fines were real. Because the threats were loud. Because the school sent emails with words like noncompliance and sanctions. Because parents called and told their kids to keep their heads down. Because professors who wanted to help did not want to lose their jobs. Fear is efficient. Shame is cheaper than a guard."

"What about your family?"

"My mother texted that God loved me and so did she. My father ignored my calls for a week. When he picked up, he only said to stay out of trouble. When I told him I couldn't get my prescription, he told me to pray on it. When I said prayer wouldn't stabilize my levels, he said that was a rude thing to say to your father. I learned silence that week."

"Tell me about the day you broke?"

"It was Tuesday." Jules's voice was steady now, as if naming it gave the memory a weight. "They had put up new signs overnight. 'Biological Use Only.' Someone had added a marker line under it that said 'Prove It.' I stood outside the bathroom, trying to decide where to go. A boy I didn't know grabbed my elbow and told me to turn around. I shook him off. He shoved me. He wasn't big, but I was tired. I slipped and hit my head on the corner of the sign. My eyebrow split. Blood ran down my face. He looked sorry for a second, then security came and escorted me to the office. The woman with the cross gave me a pamphlet about complying with state law. I asked for a bandage. She said she would pray with me. I asked again. She said prayer first."

"Did you pray?"

"No."

"What did you do?"

"I took the pamphlet. I folded it and pressed it to my eyebrow to stop the bleeding. It didn't absorb much. It just smeared the ink."

"What did the low IQ man's office say when you wrote?"

"He didn't answer. A staffer did. The staffer said the law protected vulnerable populations. They said if I had concerns I could bring them up at the next listening session. They said the low IQ man believed in personal responsibility. I wrote back and asked whose responsibility it was that my clinic closed. They didn't respond again."

"Why are you glad he is dead?"

"Because he can't sign another thing against me. Because he can't hold a leather folder and pretend there is no blood on the page. Because he can't shake hands with men who will use my body to raise money. Because he can't smile into a lens and call it love. Because low IQ men are so very mediocre and I am tired of them ruining everything for everyone just because they are so very dumb. So dumb."

"Does his death fix what was done?"

"No. The policy is still there. The desk is still in the student center. The bathroom still has that line that says prove it. My clinic is still closed. My doctor still whispers on the phone. But he is gone. One voice is quiet. That matters."

"Do you think someone will replace him?"

"Yes. There are always men lined up to hold the pen."

"Then why celebrate?"

"Because he doesn't get to watch me endure. Because he doesn't get to count me as a number. Because at least one hand that signed my life smaller is in the dirt. I am still here."

"What did you carry out of that year?"

Jules reached into the pocket of the denim jacket and pulled out a rectangle of cardstock. It was a campus pass, the photo rubbed thin until the face was gone.

"I kept this when they told me to return it," Jules said. "They said it was invalid. I said I lost it. I kept it as a key that opens nothing. I kept it to remind me the door was never locked from my side."

"And one true thing about yourself? Not about him. About you."

Jules breathed slow. "I am still building the body that is mine. Every day I add a brick. Some days I pull one out because it doesn't fit. Some days I hold the plan in my lap and cry. But the building is mine. No one else gets to draw it."

"Do you hate him?"

"Yes."

"Will you always."

"No. One day there will be too many new bricks for me to see his name. But not today."

The bulb flickered and steadied. The recorder's red light kept its small watch. I tapped the table lightly so the sound marked the end.

"Go," I said. "You have said what needed saying."

Jules stood. Their chair scraped a hard line across the floor. At the door they paused and looked back at the circle of light.

"Are you going to keep doing this?" they asked.

"Until the questions run out," I said.

They nodded once and left. The hinges groaned closed. Their steps faded. The basement took its breath again. The pipes ticked in the walls. The bleach smell settled like a thought that would not leave.

I leaned back, folded my hands, and smiled my sugar-sweet smile.

"Next," I said.

~3
The River Burns

The lightbulb swung gently on its cord, buzzing above the table like it wanted to remind me it was still there. The smell of bleach was weaker now, giving way to something damp that rose from the floor. My chair creaked when I leaned forward. I set the recorder on the table and clicked it on.

"Oh gee," I said. "I'm glad he's dead."

The door opened slow. A man stepped in with shoulders bent like the weight of something invisible pressed down on them. His clothes smelled faintly of smoke and river mud. His boots left dark prints across the concrete. He took the chair and sat heavy, like he did not trust it to hold him.

"What is your name?" I asked.

"Elias."

"All right, Elias. Who is dead?"

"The man in the suit. The one with the clean hands who signed the permits."

"What permits?"

"The ones that let them dump into the river. The ones that turned it black. The ones that took the air out of my boy's lungs."

"Tell me what happened."

He rubbed his face, and when he lowered his hands his eyes were rimmed red. "We lived by the water. My family always had. We fished, swam, washed, cooked. The river was our life. Then one morning it stank. Thick and sour, like rotten eggs. Fish floated belly-up, white eyes rolling. I told my son not to touch them. He was ten. He laughed and said, 'Dad, I know.' But he picked one up anyway. It was slick with oil. His hands burned for days."

"What did you see when the dumping began?"

"Trucks at night. Unmarked. They backed up to the banks and hissed chemicals into the water. We tried to take pictures. Men in black jackets came and told us we would be arrested for trespassing on public land. Public land, they said, while pouring poison into our river."

"What happened to your boy?"

Elias's voice broke. "He coughed. First at night. Then all day. His spit came up red. His skin broke into sores. We went to the clinic and they said it was asthma. They gave us an inhaler. It did nothing. Two months later he was in a hospital bed. Tubes everywhere. He looked at me and asked if he could still play baseball in the spring. I told him yes. I lied."

"And the man in the suit?"

"He came on television. He said the plant was clean. He said the tests showed no danger. He said the community was hysterical. He said children always get sick in winter. He smiled when he said it. He smiled while my son's lungs filled with blood."

"What did your neighbors do?"

"Some packed up and left. Those who could afford it. Most of us stayed. Where would we go? The land was cheap because of the stink. And then the company bought up empty houses. They bulldozed them and said it was to make way for progress. We knew what that meant."

"Why did no one stop it?"

"Because the company owned the sheriff. Because the company owned the newspaper. Because the company paid for the senator's campaign. Because the man in the suit signed the paper that said it was all legal."

"What did the river look like?"

Elias closed his eyes. "Thick. Oily. On some days it caught fire. Flames on the surface, dancing like carnival lights. Children stood on the bridge and watched water burn. They thought it was a trick. They laughed. We did not."

"Tell me about the night your boy died."

Elias's lips trembled. "It was late. Machines beeped. The nurse had left to get another bag. I held his hand. It was so light. He whispered, 'Dad, it's hard to breathe.' I told him to hold on. He said, 'It feels like the river is inside me.' Then he shuddered once and went still. The machine screamed. I screamed louder."

The bulb above us flickered like it could not bear to shine on the words.

"Why are you glad the man in the suit is dead?" I asked.

Elias's jaw clenched. "Because he cannot smile anymore. Because he cannot stand in front of cameras and call poison clean. Because he cannot sign another permit that kills children. Because for once, the river took him instead of us."

"Does his death bring your boy back?"

"No." His voice was flat. "My boy is in the ground. His glove is still in the closet. His bed is still made. Nothing changes that."

"Does his death heal your water?"

"No. The river still stinks. The fish still die. My neighbors still cough in the night. But his pen is gone. His hand is dirt. That matters."

"Then why glad?"

"Because at least one thief is finished. Because the man who sold our breath for money is no longer breathing himself. Because he did not die rich in a mansion but down in the mud of his own making. I am glad for that."

"What did you carry out of the fire?"

Elias reached into his jacket pocket and pulled out a small, crumpled object. It was a boy's baseball card, the edges curled and blackened.

"I found this under his pillow after the funeral," he said. "It still smells like smoke. I keep it with me. It is the only thing that still belongs to him."

"And one true thing about yourself," I asked. "Not about him. About you."

Elias's eyes glistened. "I am still his father. Even if the world burned him out of me, I am still his father. They cannot take that."

"Do you hate the man in the suit?"

"Yes."

"Will you always?"

Elias thought for a long moment. "Until the river runs clear again. Until then, yes."

The basement pressed close around us. The bulb steadied, humming like it wanted to keep the silence company.

I clicked the recorder off. Elias tucked the baseball card back into his jacket and rose. His boots scraped against the floor. At the door he stopped and looked at me.

"Will you ask more?" he said.

"Yes."

"Good. Don't stop."

He left. The hinges groaned shut. The basement sighed, pipes ticking in the walls. The smell of river mud lingered after him.

I leaned back in my chair, smoothed my skirt, and smiled the sugar smile.

"Next," I said.

The bleach smell had thinned in the basement, but the damp was still there, soaked into the concrete like something that would never dry. The bulb buzzed above me, the sound thin and steady. I set the recorder back in place, pressed the red button, and leaned forward.

"Oh gee," I said. "I'm glad he's dead."

The door opened. A woman stepped in slowly, her hands clasped in front of her stomach. She wore a faded hospital gown under a cardigan, the ties at the back knotted tight. Her eyes were hollow, the kind that had cried themselves dry. She took the chair without looking at me.

"What is your name?" I asked.

"Claire."

"All right, Claire. Who is dead?"

"The man from the boardroom. The one who said our water was safe."

"What happened to you?"

Her breath caught. "I carried two children. Neither made it past the fifth month. My doctor told me it was bad luck. My neighbor told me it was God's will. I knew it was the river. Everyone did. It smelled like bleach and gasoline, and still we drank because there was nothing else."

"What did the company say?"

"They held meetings in the school gym. Men in suits lined up under a banner that said Progress and Growth. They showed us charts. They told us the water was within safety standards. They handed out pamphlets with smiling families by a lake that did not exist here. I asked why my skin burned when I washed the dishes. They told me it was stress. I asked why the fish floated belly up. They said it was seasonal. I asked why the women on my street were losing babies. They said coincidence. They lied until the lies were the only thing left."

"What did the river look like?"

"Brown. Some mornings it shimmered purple in the sunlight, like it was wearing oil for jewelry. Froth collected on the banks in piles as high as my knees. Dogs that lapped at it died within a week. Children came home with rashes up their arms. We learned to hold our breath when we bathed. We learned not to let the water touch our lips. But how do you live without water?"

"What happened the second time you lost a child?"

Her fingers tightened together until her knuckles whitened. "I was five months along. I woke in the night with cramps so sharp I thought I was being torn open. Blood soaked the sheets. My husband carried me to the truck, and we drove with the windows down because I could not stop vomiting. At the hospital the nurses whispered. They put me in a room with no windows. I held what should have been my daughter in my hands. She was small, red, silent. I named her Grace. They took her away before the sun came up. No birth certificate. No record. Just gone."

"What did the man in the boardroom say then?"

"He went on television the next day. He said our town had an unfortunate streak of poor maternal health. He said the company was donating money for education programs. He said nothing about the river. He smiled when he said it. I wanted to reach through the screen and tear that smile off."

"Why are you glad he is dead?"

Her eyes lifted to mine, burning though dry. "Because he cannot stand in front of another mother and call her grief statistics. Because he cannot cash another check signed with blood. Because he cannot pour poison and call it progress. Because his own lungs filled with water at the end, and maybe for a second he knew what drowning feels like."

"Does his death bring your children back?"

"No. Their names are whispers in my throat. Grace. Daniel. They are not coming back."

"Does his death heal the river?"

"No. It still runs brown. The foam still piles on the banks. The company still pays its guards to keep us quiet. But he is gone, and that matters."

"Then why glad?"

"Because his signature no longer stains paper. Because he cannot buy another sheriff or silence another doctor. Because the world has one less liar with polished shoes. That is enough for tonight."

"What did you carry out of that loss?"

Claire opened her cardigan slowly. She pulled out a tiny knitted cap, pale blue, no bigger than her palm. She set it on the table.

"I made this for Daniel," she said. "It never fit him. I carry it with me so he is not forgotten. When people tell me I never had children, I hold this and know they are wrong."

"And one true thing about yourself. Not about him. About you."

Her lips trembled. "I can still sing. My voice shakes, but I sing to the empty room at night. I sing to Grace. I sing to Daniel. My songs are theirs."

"Do you hate him?"

"Yes."

"Will you always?"

Her eyes closed. "Not always. Hate takes too much air. One day I will lay it down. But not yet."

The bulb above us sputtered once and steadied. The knitted cap lay between us, fragile as breath.

"Go," I said gently. "You have said what needed saying."

Claire stood. She picked up the cap and pressed it to her chest. At the door she paused.

"Will you keep asking?"

"Yes."

"Good," she whispered. "Do not stop."

She left. The hinges whined. The basement sighed into silence again, heavy as wet stone.

I leaned back, smoothed my skirt, and let the sugar smile rise.

"Next," I said.

~4
The Eyes Taken

The basement had grown colder. Moisture clung to the walls, and the bulb swayed on its cord, buzzing louder than usual as if it did not like what was coming. I set the recorder on the table and pressed the red button. My hands folded neatly in front of me, sugar smile at the ready.

"Oh gee," I said. "I'm glad he's dead."

The door opened with a long squeal. A woman entered slowly, her steps careful, deliberate. She wore dark glasses even though the light was weak. Her cane tapped the concrete before each move forward. She felt her way into the chair, and when she sat, she kept her chin lifted, as though daring me to ask why she hid her eyes.

"What is your name?" I asked.

"Maria."

"All right, Maria. Who is dead?"

"The surgeon. The one who told me not to believe my own body."

"What happened to you?"

Her hands clenched around the handle of her cane. "I went to the clinic because I was in pain. Sharp, stabbing pain behind my eyes. I told them it felt like knives in my skull. The surgeon looked at me and smiled like I was a child. He said it was nothing. He said women exaggerate. He said my tears were hysteria. Then he leaned close and whispered that I should be grateful for his attention."

"What did he do next?"

"He cut me," she said flatly. "Without telling me why. Without asking. He said he needed to examine tissue. He said I was overreacting when I screamed. He said my nerves were fine. When I told him the pain was worse, he told me to stop being dramatic."

"What happened to your eyes?"

Maria lifted the glasses from her face. Her eyelids trembled. One iris was clouded, milky, the color of ash. The other darted side to side as if it could not settle.

"He burned them," she said. "Not with fire. With light. A laser, he called it. He said it was routine. He said it would fix me. It blinded me instead. He told the staff I was unstable when I screamed that I could no longer see clearly. They strapped me down. He laughed when I begged."

The bulb above buzzed, jittering shadows across her face.

"What did the hospital say afterward?" I asked.

"They circled their wagons. They told me complications happen. They said I should be thankful I was alive. They said I was imagining half of it. They gave me a stack of papers with fine print I could no longer read. They told me to sign. I signed. What else could I do?"

"What did you carry home from that?"

Her jaw clenched. "Scars. Scars on my eyelids, scars in my mind. And a pamphlet that told me how to live as a blind woman, as though it was inevitable, as though he had not stolen my sight."

"Why are you glad he is dead?"

Her lips curled into something between a sneer and a sob. "Because he cannot blind another woman and call it medicine. Because he cannot strap another patient down and tell her to stop being dramatic. Because he cannot smile with his white teeth and call it science when it was cruelty."

"Does his death give you back your vision?"

"No. I wake every morning to shadows. I stumble on sidewalks. I cannot see my children's faces the way I once did. Nothing brings that back."

"Does his death end the pain?"

"No. The pain still throbs. Sometimes it feels like the knives are still in my skull. But his laughter is gone. And that matters."

"Then why glad?"

"Because the world is minus one predator. Because he cannot hide behind his white coat any longer. Because his arrogance rots with him. Because at least once, the scalpel turned back on the man who wielded it."

"What do you want remembered here?"

She tilted her chin higher. "That I was not crazy. That my tears were not hysteria. That my pain was real. That he turned my body into his experiment, and when I said stop, he cut deeper."

"What is one true thing about yourself, Maria, not about him?"

Her mouth softened. "I can still sing. My voice carries where my eyes cannot. When I sing, I do not stumble. When I sing, my children hear me and know I am still here."

"Do you hate him?"

"Yes."

"Will you always?"

Her hand smoothed the cane's handle as if it were an altar. "Until my last breath, yes. I will not forgive a man who turned my world dark for his amusement."

The bulb sputtered, humming like an angry wasp. The shadows deepened on the walls.

"Go," I said gently. "You have said what needed saying."

Maria slid her glasses back on. She stood, tapping her way to the door. At the threshold she paused.

"Will you keep asking?"

"Yes."

"Good," she said, and left.

The door closed. The basement sighed, the pipes in the walls ticking like a clock. The recorder's red light glowed on.

I leaned back, folded my hands, and let the sugar smile return.

"Next," I said.

The basement was quiet again, the silence holding its breath like it did not want to be disturbed. The bulb buzzed faintly overhead, a tired sound, steady and low. I pressed the recorder's red button and leaned forward across the table.

"Oh gee," I said. "I'm glad he's dead."

The hinges moaned, and the door opened. A woman walked in slowly, her hand resting on her stomach though there was nothing left to protect. She wore a loose dress that hung awkwardly, her body thinner than it should have been. Her eyes were hollow, as if the world had stolen something more than flesh. She sat down hard, the chair squealing under her.

"What is your name?" I asked.

"Leah."

"All right, Leah. Who is dead?"

"The doctor," she said. Her voice cracked, but her eyes stayed steady. "The one who took what was mine and called it healing."

"What did he do?"

Leah looked down at her hands. They trembled against the table. "I went into the hospital for pain. Just pain. I thought it was a cyst. I thought it was something small. He came into
48

my room with a smile that did not reach his eyes. He told me I was lucky. He said he had the answer. He said he could fix me. I woke up with stitches across my stomach and an emptiness I could feel before I even opened my eyes."

"What had he done?"

"He cut me open and took my womb," Leah whispered. "Without asking. Without warning. He said it was necessary. He said it was the best thing for me. He said it was mercy."

"Was it?"

Her head snapped up, eyes sharp with fury. "No. It was theft. It was control. It was violence dressed as kindness. He did not save me. He erased me."

"What did the hospital say afterward?"

"They told me it was standard. They told me I should be grateful it was not cancer. They told me women my age did not need children anyway. They told me to rest and smile. They sent me home with a folder full of instructions about how to accept my new life."

"What did your family say?"

"My husband cried. My mother told me at least I was alive. My friends whispered behind my back, wondering if maybe I had agreed. No one wanted to believe that a doctor could cut me open without my consent. It was easier to believe I had chosen it. Easier for them. Not for me."

"What did you lose that day?"

She placed both hands on her stomach again. "I lost my future children. I lost the choice. I lost my trust in anyone who calls themselves healer. I lost the sound of my own body telling me it might still create. He turned me into a hollow thing and told me to call it health."

"Why are you glad he is dead?"

Leah's voice sharpened. "Because he cannot cut another woman while she sleeps. Because he cannot stand in another recovery room and smile while she weeps. Because he cannot erase another womb and call it progress. Because his hands are no longer steady. Because the grave keeps them still."

"Does his death give you back what he took?"

"No. I wake every morning with the same scar. I touch it and feel the emptiness inside. It is always there."

"Does his death heal your trust?"

"No. I still flinch when a nurse touches my arm. I still feel my throat close when a man in a white coat enters the room. That will not fade."

"Then why glad?"

Her hands curled into fists. "Because at least he cannot do it again. Because I can say to myself that one monster is gone. Because sometimes that has to be enough."

"What did you carry out from that day?"

She reached into her dress pocket and pulled out a crumpled hospital bracelet. The plastic was cracked, the ink faded. She set it on the table and stared at it as though it still burned.

"This," she said. "They cut it off me when I left, but I kept it. It has my name. My birthday. And under reason for admission, it says abdominal pain. Not hysterectomy. Not surgery. Just pain. That is all I went in with. That is the proof."

"And one true thing about yourself, Leah. Not about him. About you."

Her lips trembled. "I am still a mother. Even without children in my arms. I mother my friends. I mother my neighbors. I mother myself when I curl into bed and cry. They cannot take that from me. He cannot take that from me."

"Do you hate him?"

"Yes."

"Will you always?"

Her gaze fell back to the bracelet. She spoke softly. "Until the day my scar no longer aches when I breathe. Until then, yes."

The bulb above us hummed steady, the light flickering once before it calmed again. The bracelet sat between us like a witness.

"Go," I said. "You have said what needed saying."

Leah picked up the bracelet, held it tight in her fist, and stood. She hesitated at the door, her shoulders stiff.

"Will you keep asking?" she whispered.

"Yes."

"Good," she said. "Do not stop."

She left. The door closed slow behind her, the hinges sighing with her weight. The basement grew quiet again, the pipes in the wall ticking like the beat of a tired heart.

I leaned back in my chair, crossed my legs, and let the sugar smile return.

"Next," I said.

~5
The Mask Parade

The basement felt tighter than before, as if the room itself had been listening and did not like what it heard. The bulb hummed above the table. Bleach clung to the concrete like a stubborn thought. I placed the recorder where the light hit it and pressed the red button.

"Oh gee," I said. "I'm glad he's dead."

The door opened. Not one person this time. Four young men stepped in together. Their suits were new but a size too big, sleeves grazing knuckles, collars rough against their necks. Their haircuts looked like they had all asked for the same photograph. Each wore a small flag pin that caught the light when they moved. They stood in a crooked line and stared at the chair as if it might bite.

"Only one at a time," I said. "Choose."

They looked at each other. The tallest cleared his throat and sat. The other three stayed standing just behind his shoulders, like shadows that had learned to walk.

"What is your name?" I asked.

"Ryan," he said. His voice was thin but practiced, like a school pledge.

"All right, Ryan. Who is dead?"

"The Senator," he said. "Our mentor. A good man."

"What made him good?"

Ryan straightened. "He believed in order. He believed in faith. He believed in families. He defended what matters."

"Whose family?" I asked.

He frowned. "Everyone's."

"Did Ana belong to everyone's family?" I asked. "Did Jules?"

The boys behind him shifted. Ryan's eyes flicked to the recorder and back to me. "We cannot speak to individual cases."

"We are not in a press briefing," I said. "We are in a basement with a table and a light. Try again. What made him good?"

"He served his country," Ryan said.

"How?"

"He passed laws that reflected our values."

"Whose values?" I asked.

He swallowed. "The people's."

"Which people?"

54

"The majority," he said, and for the first time the word sounded unsure on his tongue.

"Tell me what you did for him," I said.

"Knocked doors. Stuffed envelopes. Drove him to events. Wrote copy. Recorded video. Helped with campus outreach."

"What did you say on campus?"

His back straightened again. "We said freedom needs fences. We said safety requires hard choices. We said responsibility is love."

"What did you say to Jules when they bled into a pamphlet because security would not give them a bandage?"

Ryan blinked. "I do not know who that is."

"You do. You saw the photo. You liked the post."

One of the boys behind him flinched. Ryan's jaw tightened. "If someone was hurt, we regret it."

"Regret is not the question," I said. "Responsibility is. Did you hand out the flyers that turned Jules into a warning?"

Ryan did not answer. His hands gripped the chair's edge until his knuckles paled.

"You," I said, looking past him to the boy on his left. "What is your name?"

"Caleb," the boy said, too quickly.

"Did you write the bathroom signs?" I asked.

Caleb's mouth opened and closed. "I designed the template. I did not decide where they went."

"So you made the knife," I said. "Someone else stabbed."

Caleb looked at the floor. The flag pin on his lapel flashed once and went dull.

I turned back to Ryan. "Do you know Claire?"

"No," he said.

"She named her children Grace and Daniel. She held Daniel when he was the size of a hand. Do you know her?"

Ryan rubbed his thumb against the seam of his pants. "We cannot be held responsible for every private tragedy."

"When the tragedies are private because your team made them untellable, you can," I said. "When your office gave out talking points that called miscarriages unfortunate events and moved on, you can."

Ryan's eyes darted to the door and back. "The Senator made policy. He did not cause misfortune."

"The permits for the river," I said. "Whose signature is at the bottom?"

"State officials," he said carefully.

"And the letters of support attached to those permits. Whose letterhead?"

He did not answer.

"Yours," I said. "His. The campaign's."

"We created jobs," Ryan said. "You have to understand the bigger picture."

"Tell me the bigger picture," I said. "Paint it for me. What does the bigger picture look like when a father is burying his son?"

Ryan opened his mouth and closed it again. The other boys stared at the bulb as if it might burn them clean.

"What did he tell you about people like Ana?" I asked.

"That girls your age needed guardrails," Ryan said. He spoke the line like he had said it many times. "That freedom without limits becomes chaos. That if the law is clear, lives will be saved."

"Whose lives?"

"The unborn," he said, with sudden confidence.

"And the born?" I asked.

He hesitated.

"The born are messy," I said. "They bleed in bathrooms. They need bandages. They need clinics. They need clean water. What did your mentor do for the born?"

Ryan licked his lips. The boys behind him took a half step back without meaning to.

"What did he teach you to do when someone cried?" I asked.

"To hold the line," Ryan said. "To stay on message. To be firm."

"What message did you use when Rose said he raped her?" I asked.

Ryan went still. Caleb's head snapped up. The third boy shifted his weight and looked ready to run.

"He was a pastor," I said. "He told girls to pray harder. He used a door with a lock. What message did you use to defend him?"

Ryan looked ill. "The Senator condemned all abuse," he said. "He issued a statement."

"A sentence is not a rescuer," I said. "Who unlocked the door? Who believed the girl? Who pulled him off the pulpit?"

No one answered me. The bulb hummed like a mechanical wasp.

"Why are you here?" I asked Ryan. "What did you think you were going to do in this room?"

He drew himself up like a man trying to fit a larger suit. "We came to speak for him. He is not here to defend himself."

"You do not need to defend the dead," I said. "You need to tell the truth. Why are you glad he is dead?"

Ryan recoiled. "I am not," he said.

"You will be," I said. "Maybe not tonight. Maybe not this year. But one day you will hear the words he taught you in your own mouth and you will taste the metal in them. You will be glad the teacher of that taste is gone."

Ryan stared at me. The boy to his right swallowed and looked away.

"What did he give you?" I asked.

"A path," Ryan said. "A job. A cause. A way to matter."

"What did it cost?"

Ryan's fingers loosened on the chair. "Friends. Time. Some sleep," he said.

"And your face in the mirror?" I asked. "Did it cost you that?"

He did not answer.

"You," I said to the third boy. "Your name."

"Evan," he said softly.

"What did you do for him?"

"I filmed," Evan said. "Clips for social. Edits for rallies. I cut the angry parts out of his opponents and looped the worst seconds."

"What did you cut out of him?" I asked.

Evan looked at Ryan. Ryan gave a tiny nod that said do not. Evan looked back at me. "Nothing," he said.

"What did he say in the car when the camera was off?"

Evan pressed his lips together. "He said numbers move people. He said keep the footage of crying mothers short because it turns the audience. He said never show empty houses unless they are tidy. He said always show flags."

"What did he say about the river?" I asked.

"He said that people in towns like that were used to tough things," Evan said. "He said they would bounce back. He said the opposition wanted to turn every sad story into a policy change. He said our job was to keep him looking strong."

"Do you think he was strong?" I asked.

Evan rubbed his palms on his pants. "He was loud," he said.

"Loud is not strong," I said. "Loud is a mask when the room is full of quiet grief."

I turned back to Ryan. "You said he gave you a way to matter. Does he still give you that in the ground?"

Ryan stared past me. "I do not know."

"What do you carry that belongs to him?" I asked.

Ryan reached into his pocket and pulled out a note card. The edges were bent soft from use. He placed it on the table. In blue ink a list of phrases stared up at us. Protect families. Respect life. Common sense. Personal responsibility. Restore order. American values.

"His lines," he said. "For interviews."

"Which of these lines can face Claire's knitted cap?" I asked. "Which can face Daniel's baseball card? Which can face Ana's stolen page?"

Ryan's chest rose and fell. "None," he said finally.

"What is one true thing about yourself?" I asked. "Not about him. About you."

He looked very young for the first time. "I wanted to help," he said. "I did not know how to do it without hurting someone else."

"Do you hate him?" I asked.

Ryan swallowed. "No," he said. Then he paused. "Maybe I will. I do not know what to do with that."

"You do not have to know tonight," I said. "You have to know this. The mask is off. The words on your card are only sounds. The people you stood over are still here."

Ryan nodded once. Behind him, Caleb took a small step to the side, as if he could move out of his own shadow. Evan kept his eyes on the table. The fourth boy had not spoken at all. He stood with his hands in fists, as if the room might charge him.

"Go," I said softly. "All of you. Bring me the next person who thinks the card can answer a mother. Then bring me someone who knows it cannot."

Ryan rose. The others moved with him. At the door he turned back.

"Are you going to keep doing this?" he asked.

"Until the questions run out," I said.

He opened his mouth to speak, closed it, and left. The door groaned shut behind them. Their footsteps faded down the hallway, uneven, like a parade that had forgotten its marching song.

The basement exhaled. The bulb steadied. The note card sat on the table, blue ink shining under the light. I picked it up, read the lines again, and slid it under the recorder.

"Next," I said.
The bulb above the table hummed its tired tune. The note card of talking points lay under the recorder where I had left it, blue ink catching the light. The bleach smell had thinned to a faint sting. I clicked the recorder on and let my voice warm like tea on a back burner.

"Oh gee," I said. "I am glad he is dead."

The door opened. One of the boys from before stood in the frame alone. He had the same suit, the same shaved sides, the same small flag pin. Without the others he looked younger, like a kid wearing his father's blazer. He stepped in and closed the door behind him. His hand stayed on the knob longer than it needed to.

"Sit," I said.

He sat. He did not touch the table. His hands rested on his knees, palms open, as if he were waiting to catch something that might fall.

"What is your name?" I asked.

"Caleb," he said. His voice was smaller without his friends close by.

"Caleb," I said. "You stood behind Ryan like a shadow. Now you are here as yourself. Who is dead?"

"The Senator," he said. "The man I worked for. The man I thought I believed."

"What did you do for him?"

"I made things," he said. "I designed. I wrote headlines. I laid out flyers. I scheduled posts. I picked photos. I chose angles. I did the look of it all."

"The bathroom signs," I said.

He closed his eyes. "Yes. I drew that font on my laptop at two in the morning. I thought I was clever. I thought I was helping."

"What did it say?"

"Biological Use Only," he said. "Then someone added a line underneath. Prove It. I did not write that part. I made the template that let it fit."

"Did you know what it would do?"

He stared at the floor. "I told myself it was just a sign. I told myself a sign cannot hurt anyone. I watched the video of Jules bleeding and I closed the tab. I said the angle made it look worse. I said the internet lies."

"What is the truth?" I asked.

"The internet was the only place that told it straight," he said. "The boy pushed. Security stalled. The woman with the cross said prayer first. Jules held a pamphlet to their face because it was all they had. I made the paper that did not absorb blood."

"What else did you make?"

He swallowed. "I built the website page for the Senator's statement after the pastor was arrested. I put a soft blue

63

behind the text. I chose a photo where the Senator's jaw looked firm. I replaced a sentence that condemned abuse with a sentence that condemned rumors. I thought it would play better. I told myself it was just one word. Rumors instead of crimes. Now I cannot stop hearing the difference."

"Did you know the girls?" I asked.

"No," he said. "But I saw them. Blurred faces on the local news. Shadows in church parking lots. Hands tied up in their own sleeves. I told myself I did not know them so I did not owe them anything. I was wrong."

"What did he teach you?" I said.

"He taught me that words can be armor," Caleb said. "He taught me that a clean font makes poison look like water. He taught me that if I am quick and confident, people will stop asking questions. He taught me that a mask can be printed and worn by a whole town."

"Are you glad he is dead?"

Caleb's mouth opened and shut like a fish trying to breathe air. "I do not know what the right answer is," he said.

"There is no right answer," I said. "There is only your answer."

He looked at the recorder as if it might tell him what to say. "Yes," he said at last. "I am glad he is dead. I am ashamed that I am glad. I am ashamed that I am ashamed. None of those help the people I hurt."

"Shame is a chair," I said. "You can sit in it. Or you can stand up and move it out of the way. What did you carry out of the building when you left the campaign?"

64

He blinked. "How did you know I left?"

"You came alone," I said. "You closed the door with your hand still on the knob. Men who are still inside rooms do not hold doors that way."

He took a breath. "I carried a hard drive," he said. "I copied the media folder. Not the donors. Not the opposition research. The folder with drafts and videos and templates. There are versions of his speeches where he tries out the cruelest lines and laughs. There are rehearsal clips where he tells a mother she is lying and then practices a frown for the camera. There are mockups of the bathroom signs that use worse words. I took all of it."

"Why?"

"Because I thought maybe one day I would need to show someone that I am not innocent," he said. "I thought maybe the truth should exist in a place he cannot control. I thought maybe a record matters more than my pride."

"What do you want this room to know?" I asked.

"That I knew," he said. "Not everything. Enough. Enough to stop. And I did not stop. Not when Ana's roommate died. Not when the river burned. Not when the pastor's statement changed. I kept trying to make the mean parts look smooth. I kept using pretty to hide harm."

"What did it cost you?"

"My face," he said. "When I look in the mirror, I see a sign. Not a man. A sign that points the wrong way."

"What brought you here?" I asked.

Caleb touched the flag pin on his lapel, then took it off and set it on the table. "Ryan said you were just a woman in a basement with a microphone and a mouth. He said it like a threat. Then he looked scared when he said it. I thought, if a woman and a mouth can scare him, I should find out why."

"Why are you glad he is dead?" I asked again.

He looked at his empty lapel. "Because without him, there is one less voice teaching me how to lie," he said. "Because he cannot pat my shoulder and call me a good soldier. Because the brand I wore does not have a living master now. It is only cloth."

"Do you think someone will take his place?"

"Yes," Caleb said. "They already have. The inbox did not go dark. The templates still load. The machine keeps turning."

"Then what do you owe the people who sat in this chair before you?" I asked.

He did not speak. He picked up the flag pin, turned it once, and set it down again.

"What do you owe Jules?" I asked.

"A bandage," he said. "And a public apology. And a job if they want one. And a room where no one checks their body at the door."

"What do you owe Claire?" I asked.

"A name on the record for Grace and Daniel," he said. "Money for filters that work. Voices louder than the company's. Faces at the meetings. Laws that deny permits, not rubber stamps."

"What do you owe Rose?" I asked.

"A new lock on every door," he said. "A list of every church that moved a predator instead of naming him. A speech that says we were wrong and means it. A number she can call that does not route her back to men who want to pray while she bleeds."

"What do you owe yourself?" I asked.

Caleb stared at the recorder. "To stop pretending that fonts are neutral," he said. "To stop using nice words to cover sharp things. To say no. To put my hands down when someone tries to place them on a keyboard for harm."

"Do you hate him?" I asked.

Caleb took a long breath and let it out. "I want to," he said. "It would be easier than hating what I did. But hate would let me off the hook. If I hate him, I can pretend that the monster was only him. I cannot do that. Not here."

"What do you carry that belongs to him?" I asked.

He reached into his jacket and pulled out a small leather card case. He slid a business card across the table. It was heavy stock. The Senator's name embossed in gold sat centered and calm.

"He handed me a stack of these the day he won his primary," Caleb said. "He told me we were going to fix the country. I believed him. I carried this card like a promise. I still carried it after I knew what we were doing. I want to put it somewhere it can hear the truth."

I set the card on top of the talking points under the recorder. The stack looked like a small altar to the shape of a lie.

"What is one true thing about yourself," I asked. "Not about him. About you."

Caleb stared at the pile. His eyes filled and cleared without spilling. "I can make words look beautiful," he said. "From now on I will only do that for the people who sit in the chair and shake when they speak."

"Will you send me the folder?" I asked.

He nodded. "Yes. I want it somewhere I cannot take it back."

The bulb above us flickered once and steadied. The room had the quiet of a held breath.

"Go," I said. "You have said what needed saying."

Caleb stood. He slid the empty card case back into his pocket. At the door he stopped and spoke without turning.

"Do you think I can make anything right?" he asked.

"Not everything," I said. "Something. Start there."

He nodded and left. The hinges whined and closed on air that felt thinner after him.

I waited. The pipes ticked. The recorder's red light blinked a slow pulse. The stack of cards and phrases sat where everyone could see them if they came close.

The door opened again without a knock. The last boy from the earlier group stepped in. He was compact, with a wrestler's neck and a stare designed to look like certainty. He shut the door with a firm hand and planted himself in the chair as if he were bracing for a collision.

"What is your name?" I asked.

"Mark," he said.

"Who is dead?"

"The Senator," he said. "The best man I ever met."

"What did you do for him?"

"I took care of problems," Mark said. "I made calls. I put out fires. I kept noise from reaching him."

"What kind of noise?" I asked.

He smiled without humor. "People like you. People who collect sad stories and try to turn them into rules."

"What did you do to Claire's letter when it came to the office?" I asked.

"Returned to sender," he said.

"What did you do when the river burned?" I asked.

"Sent a team with flags and told them to stand on the bridge for photos," he said. "We beat the opposition to the shot."

"What did you do when the pastor's arrest hit the local news?" I asked.

"Called the station manager," he said. "Bought time for a statement. Set the narrative."

"What did you do when Jules bled in the student center?" I asked.

"Called campus security and told them to remove friendly media," he said. "Then I called a friendly influencer and gave him a memo. He said the video was fake. It trended for a night."

"Are you glad he is dead?" I asked.

"No," Mark said. "I will never be glad."

"Will you be glad when your son asks you why you helped break people and you have to say the words out loud?" I asked.

Mark flinched like someone had thrown cold water at him. "I do not have a son," he said.

"You will have a question one day that feels like a son," I said. "It will stand in your doorway and ask who you were. Are you glad he is dead?"

He looked at the note card under the recorder. His jaw worked. "I believed in him," he said. "I still do."

"What did he believe in?" I asked.

"In winning," Mark said.

"What do you believe in?" I asked.

He did not answer.

"What do you carry that belongs to him?" I asked.

Mark pulled a phone from his pocket and put it on the table. The lock screen was a photo of the Senator on a stage, hands raised, confetti in the air. Mark stared at the picture like it might speak.

"You can keep a picture," I said. "You cannot keep yourself in it forever."

He picked up the phone and turned it face down. "What do you want me to say?" he asked.

"I want you to tell me the first thing that comes into your head when I say the name Claire," I said.

He pressed his lips together. "Foam on brown water," he said.

"Ana," I said.

"Paper," he said.

"Jules," I said.

"Blood on the words," he said.

"Rose," I said.

"Locked door," he said.

"Elias," I said.

"Glove in a closet," he said.

He breathed out like he had been underwater.

"Are you glad he is dead?" I asked again.

Mark stared at the face down phone. "I am glad I am not sitting next to him on a stage right now," he said. "I am glad I am here. I am not ready for more than that."

"It will do," I said. "For tonight."

He stood. He did not look at me when he left. He closed the door with a careful hand.

The basement became still. The stack under the recorder looked heavier, as if the phrases had gained weight from being spoken aloud and found empty. I slid the top card free. The gold name shone.

I smiled, sweet as candy, sharp as a lid.

"Next," I said.

~6
The Pastor's Lesson

The basement did not change, but each story left a different shape in the air. Tonight it felt heavy, as if the walls themselves sagged under the weight of secrets. The bulb swayed gently on its cord, humming its tired note. The folding chairs leaned against the wall like unused witnesses. I set the recorder on the table, clicked the red button, and folded my hands together.

"Oh gee," I said. "I am glad he is dead."

The door creaked open. A girl entered. She was older now—sixteen, maybe seventeen—but still carried herself like someone younger, smaller, pressed into corners she did not choose. Her dress was too tight at the chest and too short at the hem, as if she had been made to stay twelve while the rest of her body kept growing. She tugged at the sleeves, long enough to hide the angry red tracks on her arms. Her shoes tapped softly against the concrete as she crossed the room and sat down.

"What is your name?" I asked.

She looked at the floor. Her voice was almost a whisper. "Faith."

"All right, Faith. Who is dead?"

"The pastor," she said.

"Tell me about him."

Her shoulders rose and fell once, like a shrug too heavy to finish. "He stood at the pulpit every Sunday. He wore a robe with gold trim. His Bible was leather, edges gilded so the light caught them like fire. He told us God spoke through him. Everyone nodded. Everyone said amen. Everyone trusted him."

"And you?" I asked.

"I was twelve," she said. "I thought he was God."

"What did he do?"

Her hands pulled tighter at her sleeves. She would not look at me. "He told me God had chosen me for a secret blessing. He said I was special. He said not to tell anyone or the blessing would be taken away. Then he locked the office door and told me to bow my head."

"What happened in that room?"

Her lips parted. She swallowed hard. "He touched me. He pressed me into the desk. He said God wanted me to stay still. He said my tears were holy water. He said the pain meant I was being purified."

The bulb flickered. The basement seemed to shrink.

"What did you say?" I asked.

"I said no," she whispered. "I cried. He told me to pray harder. He said if I prayed enough, the hurt would turn to light. He said girls are meant to bleed so the world can be clean."

"What did you do after?"

"I went home. I washed until my skin burned. My mother asked why I was red, and I said it was sunburn. She laughed and said I should wear longer sleeves."

"Did you tell her?"

Faith shook her head quickly. "No. I tried once. I said the pastor touched me. She slapped my mouth and told me never to say that again. She said he was a man of God. She said girls lie. She said I should pray for forgiveness for even thinking such a thing."

"What about your father?"

"He worked nights. He barely came to church. When I tried to tell him, he told me to respect my elders and mind my manners. He said girls with dirty thoughts bring shame on their families. He said the pastor was kind enough to guide me."

"And the congregation?"

Faith gave a bitter laugh. "They adored him. They called him shepherd. They brought him pies and casseroles. They gave him money for new robes. They stood when he entered, like he was a king. If I had stood up and screamed what he did, they would have covered their ears and shouted hymns until my words disappeared."

"So you were alone," I said.

"Yes," she said. "Completely."

"What did you do with the pain?"

She lifted her sleeves just enough for the scars to show. Thin white lines, angry red welts, some fresh, some old. "I cut," she said. "With scissors, with razor blades, with shards of glass. It was the only time I controlled the blade. The only time the hurt was mine. If I opened my skin, at least I decided where. At least I decided when."

"Why?" I asked softly.

"Because it was the only proof I had that I was real," she said. "He told me my body was not mine. The cuts said otherwise. They said this arm belongs to Faith. This pain belongs to Faith. He cannot take this from me."

The bulb above us swung slightly, shadows crawling across her face.

"Why are you glad he is dead?" I asked.

She exhaled a sharp breath. Her eyes were dark, fierce, even through the tears. "Because no more girls will walk into his office thinking they are safe. Because no more girls will be told to bow their heads while he locks the door. Because no more girls will carry the sound of his voice calling it holy. Because finally the prayers stop at him instead of at us."

"Does his death erase what he did?"

"No," she said. "I still see the desk when I close my eyes. I still smell the leather of his Bible. I still wake up sweating when the floor creaks like a door locking. Nothing erases that."

"Does his death heal your scars?"

"No," she whispered. "But at least the blade is only mine now, not his hands."

"Then why glad?"

She tugged at her sleeve again. "Because when I walk past the church, I do not see his shadow in the window. Because when I hear hymns, I do not hear his voice above them. Because he cannot call my tears holy again. Because the pulpit is empty and the office is closed. That is enough."

"What did you carry out from that church?"

Her lips trembled. "A Bible," she said. "But not whole. I tore it apart, page by page. I ripped Psalms first because he made me read them while he touched me. Then the Gospels. Then Revelation. I tore until it was silent. I carried the cover out under my dress. I burned the rest in the woods."

"Why keep the cover?"

"To remind me," she said. "That the words were mine to break. Not his."

The silence stretched long. I let it. Her breathing steadied as if the telling itself was a kind of cut, releasing something she had carried too long.

"One true thing about yourself," I said at last. "Not about him. About you."

Her eyes lifted, uncertain, then firm. "I can sing," she said. "Even if my throat shakes. Even if my voice cracks. I sing in the shower. I sing in the woods. I sing where no one can stop me. My songs are mine."

I leaned forward. "Sing one line for me."

She hesitated. Her lips parted. A thin, wavering note spilled into the basement, barely louder than the bulb's hum. It carried no words, just sound, fragile but unbroken. The walls seemed to listen. The pipes stilled. Even the light went quiet.

She stopped and pressed her hands to her mouth. "That is all," she whispered.

"It is enough," I said.

"Do you hate him?"

"Yes," she said. The word came quick.

"Will you always?"

She thought for a moment. "No," she said softly. "One day hate will be too heavy. But today I will carry it gladly."

The bulb flickered once and steadied.

"Go," I said gently. "You have said what needed saying."

Faith rose. She tugged her sleeves down, covering the scars again. At the door she paused and looked back at me.

"Will you keep asking?"

"Yes."

"Good," she said. Her voice was still small, but it carried. "Do not stop."

The door closed behind her. The basement breathed out, the silence thick with hymns unspoken. I reached for the recorder, the red light blinking steady.

I crossed my legs, leaned back in the chair, and let the sugar smile curve across my face.

"Next," I said.

~7
The Riot of Silence

The basement smelled of sweat tonight, though no one had been here long enough to leave it. The bulb buzzed, its light trembling as if it remembered crowds. I set the recorder down, pressed the red button, and leaned into the silence.

"Oh gee," I said. "I am glad he is dead."

The door scraped open. A young man stepped in, shoulders hunched, hood pulled tight over his head though the room was cold. His sneakers were scuffed, the soles still marked with something dark—dirt, or blood. His hands were wrapped in gauze that had already bled through. He lowered himself into the chair slowly, wincing as if his ribs still hurt.

"What is your name?" I asked.

"Malik."

"All right, Malik. Who is dead?"

"The officer," he said. "The one who gave the order. The one who said sweep them clean."

"What happened?"

His laugh was short, bitter. "We gathered on Main Street. Twenty of us at first, then fifty, then a hundred. We had signs, chants, voices. That was all. We wanted them to see us, to hear us. We wanted to say stop killing us, stop choking us, stop treating us like noise. They brought helmets, shields, batons. They called themselves order."

"What did you see first?"

"The line," Malik said. His hands curled on his knees. "Rows of black armor, visors down, clubs ready. We shouted, they did not answer. Someone banged a drum. Someone else lit a flare. The air filled with smoke. Then the officer lifted his hand. Just one hand. He dropped it. They charged."

"What did they do?"

"Hit," Malik said flatly. "Everything. Heads, backs, legs. People fell like dominoes. The sound was worse than the sight. Sticks on bone. Screams turning to grunts when the air went out. They dragged bodies to the curb and zip-tied hands so tight fingers went blue. They shoved girls into vans. They knocked old men to the ground and laughed when they couldn't get up."

"Where were you?"

"In the middle," he said. "I raised my arms. I shouted peaceful. I shouted rights. The baton hit my ribs and I swallowed the word. I went down. A boot pressed my face to the pavement. I remember the taste of asphalt, bitter and hot. My cheek burned. I heard my friend Keisha screaming. Then I did not hear her anymore."

"What happened to Keisha?"

Malik's jaw clenched. "They dragged her. I saw her hair pulled tight in a fist. Her sign fell in the street. It said Silence is Violence. They trampled it until only Silence was left."

"What did the officer say?"

"He walked down the line with his baton tapping shields like a drum major. He said sweep them clean. He said the city belongs to order. He said the rest of us were filth. He said sweep."

The bulb flickered, shadows darting across the walls.

"Why are you glad he is dead?" I asked.

"Because his baton is buried with him," Malik said. His voice shook. "Because his orders rot in the ground. Because no more kids will feel their bones break under his smile. Because he cannot sweep another street clean when the dirt was never us."

"Does his death heal your ribs?"

"No. Every breath still stabs. Laughter still hurts. Sleeping on my side still hurts."

"Does his death free your friends?"

"No. Keisha is still locked up. Others still wait for court dates. Some already have records that will follow them forever. Nothing frees them yet."

"Then why glad?"

Malik's hands trembled. "Because the silence he ordered is broken now. Because we can shout his name in anger instead of fear. Because the ground does not follow commands."

"What did you carry out from that night?"

He reached into his hoodie and pulled out a strip of cardboard, bent and torn. On it, black letters smeared by rain still read half a phrase: "Silence is—." The rest was gone.

"This," he said. "Keisha's sign. I picked it up after they dragged her. I keep it because the words are not finished. I keep it because I can."

"One true thing about yourself, Malik. Not about him. About you."

His eyes glistened. "I still speak," he said. "They broke my ribs. They bruised my lungs. They wanted me quiet. But I still speak. I still chant. My throat is mine."

"Do you hate him?"

"Yes."

"Will you always?"

He hesitated. His fingers stroked the cardboard edge. "Not always," he said. "One day the chants will be louder than his name. But today I do."

The bulb above us hummed like it wanted to join. The sign fragment lay between us, half a sentence still burning.

"Go," I said. "You have said what needed saying."

Malik rose slowly, pressing a hand to his ribs. At the door he paused.

"Will you keep asking?"

"Yes."

"Good," he said. His voice was soft, but it carried. "That is the only way the silence loses."

The door closed. The basement exhaled. The bulb swayed once and steadied.

I leaned back in my chair, crossed my legs, and let the sugar smile sharpen.

"Next," I said.

The basement walls felt closer tonight, as if they had leaned in to listen harder. The bulb above the table buzzed faint, its filament glowing the color of old paper. I set the recorder where the light struck it, pressed the red button, and folded my hands.

"Oh gee," I said. "I am glad he is dead."

The door opened. A woman stepped in slowly, her shoes worn flat, her coat hanging loose around her shoulders. Her hair was streaked with gray, though she could not have been more than forty. She clutched something wrapped in cloth, pressed close to her chest. She sat carefully in the chair, as if lowering herself into a pew.

"What is your name?" I asked.

"Lorraine."

"All right, Lorraine. Who is dead?"

"The cop," she said. Her voice cracked. "The one who shot my boy."

"Tell me what happened."

84

She unwrapped the cloth slowly. Inside was a baseball cap, faded red, the brim bent. She set it on the table, smoothing it as if it were fragile.

"He was seventeen," she said. "His name was Jordan. He had just gotten his license. He was driving my car, the one with the dent in the back door. He had the radio up too loud, singing. They pulled him over. They said his taillight was out. It wasn't. I checked the next morning. Both worked fine."

"What did the officer do?"

"He told Jordan to step out of the car. My boy said, 'Yes, sir.' He did everything right. Hands on the wheel, wallet on the dash, no sudden moves. The cop kept his hand on his gun the whole time. He said, 'Do you have anything I should know about?' Jordan said no. He said again, 'Step out of the car.' Jordan reached for the seatbelt. That was all. The cop fired. Three shots. One to the chest, two to the side. My boy fell halfway out of the car. The radio was still playing."

"What did you do when you heard?"

"My neighbor called. She said there were sirens at the corner. I ran barefoot. The tape was already up. The lights were flashing. They would not let me through. I could see him on the ground. His shirt was red, darker than the cap. I screamed his name. They told me to stay back. They said it was procedure. They let him bleed in the street while they wrote notes."

"What did the officer say?"

Lorraine's hands tightened around the brim of the cap. "He said he thought Jordan had a gun. He said the seatbelt looked like a weapon. He said he feared for his life. He said

85

the words like they were a shield. Every word polished, rehearsed. He never looked at me."

"What happened after?"

"They opened an investigation. They said it would be thorough. They said it would be independent. They put the officer on paid leave. Six months later, they said it was justified. They said the body camera footage was inconclusive. They said the dashcam was blocked by a tree. They said no charges. They said move on."

"Did they ever say your boy's name?"

Her eyes filled. "No. They called him 'the suspect.' They called him 'the driver.' They never said Jordan. They never said he liked fried chicken on Sundays. They never said he wanted to be a mechanic. They never said he could sing better than the radio he played too loud. They erased him with silence."

"What did your community do?"

"They marched. They carried signs with his face. They shouted his name. They filled the streets. The police blocked them, too. They used gas. They said it was unlawful assembly. They said the crowd was violent. My boy's picture in the air was called violence. Their bullets were called justice."

"Why are you glad the officer is dead?"

Lorraine lifted her chin. "Because he will never point his gun at another boy who looks like mine. Because he will never stand in a courtroom and say he feared for his life while my son lay buried. Because he will never polish his badge in the morning and call it honor while it dripped with blood.

86

Because the ground has claimed him, and the ground cannot be scared."

"Does his death bring Jordan back?"

Her eyes closed. "No. My boy is still gone. His room is still empty. His shoes are still by the door where he left them. Nothing brings him back."

"Does his death heal your grief?"

"No," she whispered. "Grief is a river. It keeps flowing. It fills every room. I drown in it every night."

"Then why glad?"

"Because grief is lighter when the killer is not smiling in the daylight," she said. "Because at least one gun is quiet. Because his silence is permanent now."

"What did you carry out from that night?"

She placed her hand on the cap. "This," she said. "It fell into the street when they lifted him. I pushed past the tape and grabbed it before they stopped me. Blood on the brim. I washed it, but the stain stayed. I keep it as proof. I keep it as his voice. When I hold it, I hear him singing off-key in my car."

"One true thing about yourself, Lorraine. Not about him. About you."

Her lips trembled. "I am still Jordan's mother," she said. "Even if the world tried to erase his name, I say it every morning. I say it to the air. I say it so loud the walls cannot forget. I am his mother."

"Do you hate the officer?"

"Yes," she said. Her voice was sharp, clean.

"Will you always?"

She looked at the cap. Her fingers smoothed the brim again and again. "Until the day I die," she said. "Hate is all that keeps the river from swallowing me. I will hate him until I see my boy again."

The bulb above us buzzed steady. The basement was silent except for her breath.

"Go," I said gently. "You have said what needed saying."

Lorraine stood. She picked up the cap and pressed it against her chest. At the door she turned back.

"Will you keep asking?"

"Yes."

"Good," she said. Her voice cracked, but it carried. "Keep asking until they hear us."

The door closed. The basement held the echo of her words. The bulb swung once and steadied.

I leaned back, crossed my legs, and let the sugar smile rise again.

"Next," I said.

~8
The Border that Breaks

The basement smelled of damp earth tonight, as if something outside had seeped in. The bulb swung gently, its light casting shadows like bars across the table. I set the recorder down, pressed the red button, and folded my hands.

"Oh gee," I said. "I am glad he is dead."

The door opened. A boy entered. Thin, maybe thirteen, maybe younger, though the hollows under his eyes made him look older. His clothes hung loose, donated things. His shoes were torn at the toes. He moved quietly, like someone trained not to draw attention. He sat in the chair without shifting it, without a sound.

"What is your name?" I asked.

He hesitated. His fingers curled against his knees. "Mateo."

"All right, Mateo. Who is dead?"

"The man in the suit," he said. His voice was dry, almost hoarse. "The one who wrote the policy. The one who said we had to be separated."

"Tell me what happened."

Mateo's hands clenched tighter. "We crossed at night. My mother carried my little sister. We walked through the river. It was cold, strong. My sister cried. My mother told her to be quiet, to hold on. We were caught on the other side. Lights blinded us. Men shouted. Dogs barked. They pulled us into trucks."

"What happened then?"

"They took us to a place with white walls and fences inside. They called it a facility. It was cages. Chain-link. Concrete floors. The air smelled like bleach and sickness. They told my mother to go one way, me another. I screamed. I grabbed her arm. They pulled me off. They said it was policy."

"Where did you go?"

"To a cage with other boys. They gave us thin blankets, silver like foil. The floor was hard and cold. We slept side by side, shoulder to shoulder, heads on our shoes. The lights never turned off. The noise never stopped. My mother was gone."

"What did they feed you?"

"Sometimes a sandwich, sometimes nothing. The bread was hard. The water tasted like metal. When I asked for more, they said, 'Be grateful.' Some boys cried all night. Guards told them to shut up. Some stopped crying. That was worse."

"What happened to your sister?"

His eyes filled. He shook his head. "I do not know. My mother said she was sick before. I do not know if she made it."

"What did the man in the suit say?"

"He went on TV. He said the law was clear. He said family separation was a deterrent. He said children would be safer in government custody. He said we were criminals. He said it with a smile. He never came to the cages. He never slept on the floor."

"What did the guards call you?"

"Aliens. Animals. Invaders." His jaw clenched. "But we were just hungry. Just tired. Just people."

"Why are you glad he is dead?"

Mateo looked up for the first time, eyes dark and sharp. "Because he cannot write another law that tears children from their mothers. Because he cannot stand behind a podium and say we deserve cages. Because he cannot smile while we cry. Because the dirt he feared is the dirt that covers him now."

"Does his death bring your family back?"

"No. My mother is still gone. My sister—I do not know. I may never know."

"Does his death heal your nights on the floor?"

"No. I still feel the concrete in my bones. I still dream of cages. I still wake cold."

"Then why glad?"

"Because no other boy should be told to sleep on stone. Because no other girl should be taken from her mother. Because the policy dies with him, at least for today."

"What did you carry out from that place?"

Mateo reached into his pocket. He pulled out a strip of foil blanket, crumpled, dirty. He set it on the table. "This," he said. "I tore it off before they released me. I keep it so I do not forget. It is loud when you touch it. It sounds like the nights when no one slept."

"One true thing about yourself, Mateo. Not about him. About you."

He was quiet for a long time. Then he said, "I survived. They tried to make me a number. They tried to erase my face. But I survived. That is mine."

"Do you hate him?"

"Yes."

"Will you always?"

Mateo's fingers touched the foil. "No," he said softly. "One day I will not. Hate is heavy. But today I carry it, and it keeps me warm."

The bulb buzzed steady. The foil caught the light, a flicker of silver in the dim room.

"Go," I said gently. "You have said what needed saying."

Mateo stood. He tucked the foil back into his pocket. At the door he paused, one hand on the frame.

"Will you keep asking?" he said.

"Yes."

He nodded once, sharp and sure, and slipped out. The door closed. The basement filled again with the silence of absence. The bulb swayed once and steadied.

I leaned back, crossed my legs, and let the sugar smile rise again.

"Next," I said.
The basement still smelled faintly of earth and cold metal after the boy left, but now another scent seemed to creep in—dust, old paper, the faint mildew of apartments long abandoned. The bulb buzzed above, swaying on its cord like it remembered drafts from streets with broken windows. I pressed the red button on the recorder and folded my hands again.

"Oh gee," I said. "I am glad he is dead."

The door opened slowly this time. A woman entered, maybe thirty, but her face was worn, lines carved too deep for her age. She carried a canvas grocery bag crumpled against her chest. Inside it I saw paper notices, envelopes with red stamps, folded letters. She sat down, the chair groaning under her weight, though she herself was thin.

"What is your name?" I asked.

"Danielle."

"All right, Danielle. Who is dead?"

"The banker," she said. "The one who owned the building, though he never set foot inside. The one who told the company to raise the rent until the numbers looked pretty on his chart."

"Tell me what happened."

Her lips pressed together, then opened. "I lived on 12th Street, third floor. Two rooms. It was not much, but it was mine. I had a job at the diner down the block. My daughter had a bed by the window. We could see the church steeple, the pigeons nesting under the bell. Rent was six hundred a month. I could manage that. Then one day, a letter came. New management, new owner. Rent was going up. Nine hundred. Then twelve hundred. They said the neighborhood was improving. They said the market was hot."

"Could you pay?"

"No," Danielle said. Her fingers tightened on the bag. "I tried. I worked double shifts. I skipped meals. I begged the office. They shrugged. They said it was policy. When I fell behind two months, they taped the notice to my door. Big red letters: EVICTION."

"What did you do?"

"I called the number on the letter. I asked for mercy. A man answered. His voice was smooth, polite. He said, 'Business is business. You are not a person, you are a tenant. The unit will earn more if you leave.' He said, 'We do not negotiate with loss.' Then he hung up."

"What happened next?"

"They came with locks. They told me I had twenty minutes. I packed what I could. Clothes, photographs, my daughter's drawings. I left the couch, the bed, the table. I left the home we made. They tossed us onto the sidewalk. My daughter cried until she lost her voice. I told her it was an adventure, but she knew I was lying."

"Where did you go?"

"A shelter. A church basement. Sometimes the car. I washed uniforms in bathrooms, brushed her teeth with bottled water. We slept with our heads together to stay warm. She asked when we were going home. I had no answer."

"What did the banker say then?"

"He smiled on TV," Danielle said bitterly. "He said investments were thriving. He said properties were performing. He said evictions were a sign of growth. He said the market was healthy. He never said my daughter's name. He never saw her cry."

"Why are you glad he is dead?"

Her eyes sharpened. "Because he cannot put another mother on the street for profit. Because he cannot raise another rent until the floor disappears. Because he cannot turn families into figures on a balance sheet. Because the dirt he made us sleep on is the dirt that keeps him now."

"Does his death return your home?"

"No," she whispered. "The building is still gone to me. My daughter's window is someone else's now."

"Does his death stop the market?"

"No. The market still feeds. Other men still count their profits."

"Then why glad?"

"Because one fewer mouth eats at our table," she said. "Because one less smile smirks over our hunger. Because for once, the scales tip a fraction toward us."

"What did you carry out from your home?"

Danielle reached into the bag. She pulled out a folded paper, yellowed and bent. She set it on the table. "This," she said. "It is the eviction notice. The one they taped to my door. I keep it because it is proof. Proof they did this. Proof we did not leave by choice. Proof my daughter did not imagine it."

"One true thing about yourself, Danielle. Not about him. About you."

Her hand smoothed the paper. Her eyes lifted. "I am still a mother," she said. "Even without a roof. Even without a bed. I am still her mother. They cannot take that."

"Do you hate him?"

"Yes."

"Will you always?"

She thought, her eyes tracing the red letters on the paper. "Not forever," she said slowly. "Hate is rent I cannot afford. But for now, I pay it gladly."

The bulb above buzzed, casting shadows over the paper, the word EVICTION burning bright in the dim light.

"Go," I said. "You have said what needed saying."

Danielle folded the notice carefully, slid it back into her bag, and rose. At the door she turned.

"Will you keep asking?"

"Yes."

She nodded once, firm. "Then maybe one day the answers will change."

The door closed behind her. The basement breathed, the silence heavier than before. The bulb swayed once and steadied.

I leaned back in my chair, crossed my legs, and let the sugar smile curl.

"Next," I said.

~9
The *Unseen* Freedom

The basement was quieter than usual, though the silence carried its own static, as if invisible wires had been strung through the air. The bulb buzzed above, trembling, throwing nervous shadows across the concrete walls. I set the recorder down, pressed the red button, and leaned into the hush.

"Oh gee," I said. "I am glad he is dead."

The door opened. A young man stepped in, thin but wiry, his eyes hollow with sleeplessness. He wore a faded delivery jacket, the logo half-peeled from the fabric. A phone bulged in his pocket, buzzing even here, in this basement where no orders should reach. He ignored it, though his hand twitched toward it like muscle memory. He lowered himself into the chair, his knees bouncing, the rest of him too still.

"What is your name?" I asked.

"Luis."

"All right, Luis. Who is dead?"

He exhaled sharply, a bitter laugh without humor. "The man who wrote the code. The one who built the system. The one who turned people into numbers and cages into profit."

"Tell me what happened."

Luis rubbed his palms against his thighs, eyes fixed on the table. "I worked for the app. Everyone did. Food delivery, packages, rides. At first they said it was freedom. Be your own boss, they said. Choose your hours. But the app chose for me. Every job tracked. Every pause measured. If I stopped too long, my rating dropped. If my rating dropped, I stopped eating. It was chains you couldn't see, but they were chains all the same."

"What did the app do?"

"It watched. Always. GPS on, camera on, mic on. I was a dot on a map. Customers could see me crawling across their screens. The company said it made people feel safe. Safe for them, not me. If I took a wrong turn, I was punished. If I missed a call, I was punished. If I complained, I was punished. The algorithm was my boss. Cold. Silent. Absolute."

"What happened when you fell behind?"

Luis's hands clenched. "One day I got sick. Fever. Couldn't finish my route. My phone buzzed all night—alerts, penalties, warnings. The next morning, my account was suspended. No human voice. Just code. I begged for help. A chat bot told me to try harder. I stared at the screen until I wanted to smash it, but if I smashed it, I had no way back in. They make you love the chain that strangles you."

"Who wrote this system?"

"The man in the suit," Luis said flatly. "The founder. The genius, they called him. He never rode a bike in the rain. He never stood outside a locked bathroom because time was money. He sat in glass towers and tweaked the code until our

99

lives bled into his spreadsheets. He said it was innovation. He said it was disruption. He said we were free."

"And were you free?"

Luis laughed bitterly. "Free to starve. Free to collapse. Free to die on the street and be replaced in seconds. The app did not care. The algorithm did not pause. People called it convenience. For us, it was a cage without bars."

The bulb above us flickered, shadows slicing across the walls like latticework.

"Why are you glad he is dead?" I asked.

"Because the machine has no master now," Luis said. "Because his hand will never again twist the code tighter. Because he cannot polish his image with our broken backs. Because the grave cannot run a program."

"Does his death end the app?"

"No," Luis admitted. "It runs on its own now, like a ghost. Other men will feed it. But without him, it stutters. Without him, the story changes. He cannot rewrite the script again."

"What did you carry out from this life?"

Luis reached into his pocket. He pulled out his cracked phone, the screen webbed with fractures, the case covered in stickers peeling away. He set it on the table. It buzzed once, faint, as if still alive.

"This," he said. "My leash. My prison. My proof. I keep it to remind me I was never free, but I was never a machine either. I was human, even when the screen said otherwise."

"One true thing about yourself, Luis. Not about him. About you."

Luis's lips tightened, then eased. "I am more than the numbers they gave me. More than a rating. More than five stars or three strikes. I am flesh, blood, hunger, breath. I am alive."

"Do you hate him?"

"Yes."

"Will you always?"

Luis's hand hovered over the phone. "No," he said. "One day the hate will fade, like the battery dying. But until then, I let it burn."

The bulb hummed steady. The phone buzzed again, faint, then fell silent.

I was about to end the session when Luis shifted in his chair. His voice dropped lower.

"There is more," he said.

"What more?"

He met my eyes. "The algorithm was only half of it. When I could not pay rent, when the app cut me off, I stole food. Just bread. Just milk. They caught me. The code fed me into another system. Court. Jail. Bars this time, not just lines of code. They said it was justice. It was profit."

"What happened in jail?"

Luis's jaw clenched. "They processed me like cattle. Numbers, fingerprints, mugshot. They called me Inmate, not Luis. They locked me in a cell with three others, concrete walls, steel bed. They gave us jobs. Laundry. Kitchen. Pennies an hour. Corporations bought our labor. They said it taught us responsibility. It was slavery with paperwork."

"Who controlled this?"

"The warden. The contracts. The companies. But behind it all, the same man. The same system. The banker who loved profit. The coder who loved data. Different names, same machine. We were bodies filling beds, filling quotas, filling pockets."

"What did you see there?"

Luis's eyes darkened. "Men broken. Some never left. Sentences stretched because the company needed them longer. They failed parole because the beds had to stay full. Guards beat them for sport. Cameras blinked from the corners, recording everything but justice. The food was mold. The water was brown. We were not people. We were revenue."

"Why are you glad he is dead?"

Luis leaned forward, voice sharp. "Because the machine lost its architect. Because the one who saw our chains as numbers is gone. Because he cannot tighten the screws anymore. Because the grave pays no dividends."

"Does his death free those still inside?"

"No. They are still there. They will be there tomorrow."

"Does his death erase the code?"

"No. The code runs. The prisons fill. The profit grows."

"Then why glad?"

Luis's eyes blazed. "Because hate is heavy, but it is lighter when the man who built the cage cannot breathe. Because somewhere a bed is empty tonight. Because somewhere an algorithm stutters. Because his silence is one less order we must obey."

"What did you carry out from prison?"

He pulled something from his jacket pocket—a cloth patch, frayed at the edges, with numbers stamped in faded black. He set it next to the phone.

"This," he said. "My number. They stitched it on my chest. They thought it would erase my name. I tore it off when I left. I keep it to remind me I am not a digit. I am not code. I am Luis."

"One true thing about yourself," I said again.

His voice steadied. "I am still a man. Not a profile. Not a prisoner. A man."

The bulb swung once, its light cutting across the table, illuminating the phone and the patch—two prisons, digital and physical, side by side.

"Go," I said gently. "You have said what needed saying."

Luis stood. He picked up the patch, but left the phone on the table. At the door he paused.

"Will you keep asking?"
"Yes."

He nodded once, sharp. "Then maybe one day the machine will break."

The door closed. The basement hummed, the bulb buzzing like an old wire straining under weight. The phone lay on the table, silent now, dead or only pretending.

I leaned back in my chair, crossed my legs, and let the sugar smile curl across my lips.

"Next," I said.

~10
The Ghost at the Table

The basement was colder that night. Not the kind of cold
that comes from winter or damp concrete, but the kind that
seeps from within, the chill of something unwelcome pressing
against the skin. The bulb above swayed gently though the
air was still. I placed the recorder on the table, its red light
blinking as if in warning.

"Oh gee," I said. "I am glad he is dead."

The door groaned. But no footsteps followed. Instead the
hinges creaked as though pushed by a hand I could not see.
The chair opposite mine slid across the floor, slow,
deliberate, scraping metal against concrete. It stopped at the
table's edge. Then the air shifted.

He sat.

Not like the others, not with flesh alive and breath hot. His
body was pale, waxen, bloated in places, sunken in others.
The suit clung to him, stained, torn, the fabric stiff with dirt.
His face sagged where bugs had burrowed, one eye gone, the
other milky but restless. His lips pulled back, dry and
cracked, yet somehow still able to shape words. His smell
filled the room—rot, damp wood, ash.

I folded my hands tighter. "Who are you?"

His voice rasped, broken but clear enough. "Policy," he said. "Order. Protection. Acceptable losses."

"No," I said. "Who are you?"

His jaw twitched. "I am the man they buried. The one you all are glad is dead."

"Why are you here?"

"To defend," he whispered. "To explain. To remind you the world is safer because of me."

"Tell me, then. What did you do?"

"I kept the streets clean. I kept the country safe. I signed orders. I made decisions. Hard decisions. Necessary decisions. There is no mercy in leadership. There is only survival. You call it cruelty. I call it discipline."

"Talk plain," I said. "Tell me about the boy in the house with the oven. Tell me about the girl with paint under her nails. Tell me who pressed the button."

His milky eye darted like a shutter. "Collateral," he said. "Intelligence suggested insurgents. That house had a signal. It was a node. The strike disrupted a cell. The boy was unfortunate."

"Unfortunate," I repeated. "Not a name. Not bread in an oven. Not a mother who whistled at onions. Unfortunate."

He breathed, a dry hiss. "War makes monsters. I did what leaders must do. No one remembers the votes not taken, the orders signed quietly. They remember only the explosion. This is the language of nations."

"You use a map to hide a family," I said. "You draw a circle and fill it in with ash. You call it protection. You call it discipline. What did you call the sound of a child screaming under his roof?"

He closed his mouth. For a long moment nothing moved but the bulb and the whisper of pipes. "Necessary," he said finally, and the word sounded like a rusted hinge.

"What of the girl the pastor took into his office?" I asked. "You sat with her story folded under your notes and you decided the church mattered more than a child. You called silence a community's strength. You called reputation protection. Whose salvation was that?"

His mouth tightened. "A scandal can topple institutions. Chaos follows noise. A faith eroded can break entire neighborhoods. I preserved stability."

"By preserving his pulpit you preserved his access to children," I said. "You put your stamp on his quiet. You weighed the girl's body in your ledger and found the columns thin."

He made a soft sound that could have been a laugh or a cough. "Someone must make trade-offs. Someone must be willing to bear the burden of unpleasant outcomes."

"That is your argument," I said. "But you call bearing the burden a virtue and call being held accountable cowardice." I leaned in. "Did you ever see their faces before you signed?"

He lifted his remaining eye to mine, and in that glassy pupil there was a sliver of something like memory. "Faces blur," he said. "Numbers do not. Numbers make decisions clean."

"Clean," I mocked. "Clean hands are always the ones with gloves. The blood is under the gloves."

He shifted, the chair creaking. "I am not without memory. I have nights. I do not sleep easily."

"Do you dream?" I asked.

"Sometimes," he whispered. "I dream of hearing names. Names I have told to paper and to cameras. Sometimes the rhythm gets to me. I wake and there are letters on my chest. I am tired."

"Of what?" I demanded.

"Of justification," he said. "Of answering when people demand moral clarity. I wanted to make a country efficient. I wanted to make it survive storms. I thought if I made systems strong enough, no one would starve. I thought markets could feed hunger. I thought policy could fix everything."

"And it did what?" I asked. "Who fed while you balanced ledgers?"

He looked down at his hands, which were more like old maps folded into themselves than any human palms. "You think I liked it?" His laugh leached the warmth from the room. "Do you think I enjoyed the telegrams at three in the morning? Do you think I liked the sound of an aide saying casualty numbers like inventory? I told them to be precise. Precision comforts investors. Precision calms committees."

"Then tell me this," I said. "When they counted the children, when they counted the mothers, when they turned human bodies into line items, did you ever once put your pen down and go find the mothers yourself?"

For a long minute his mouth did not move. Then, slow as a fault-line, he said, "No."

"No," I echoed. "You did not. You sent reports. You wrote statements. You visited TV studios. You called it leadership. You made a career out of distance."

He flinched like a struck thing. "Distance is necessary," he said. "Distance preserves the center."

"What center?" I asked. "The center of your profit? The center of your ego? The center of the building in which you dine?"

He opened his mouth and closed it. Then he said, quieter, "The center we promised them: safety. Prosperity. Order."

"And order for whom?" I pressed. "Because order for those you benefit looks a lot like cages for the rest."

He tried to smile. The dead do not make good smiles. "You will not find a politician who admits to cruelty by design," he said. "They will say difficult choices were made. They will say the outcomes were regrettable. They will dress it in language about balance."

"Balance," I said. "What did you balance when you signed the policy that filled cages and kept children sleeping on concrete? Which ledger did you open to see which life to take?"

His remaining eye darted away. For the first time his voice frayed. "We used models. We used projections. The model showed deterrence. The model showed fewer crossings. The model showed economic benefit. We fed the model data and trusted it."

"You trusted a model more than a mother's face," I said. "You decided the geometry of grief. The model told you people were numbers. Numbers have no faces. But people do. Men like you forget that until a child's shoe sits on a table in a kitchen and nothing else fits where it used to be."

He inhaled, and for an instant the air smelled of something like regret. "I did not mean to make suffering my art," he said. "I thought I could contain it."

"Contain?" I said. "You contained it in cells and spreadsheets and PR scripts."

He looked at the recorder as if it might speak for him. "If I had to do it again," he mumbled, "I would still sign."

"You would still sign," I repeated. "After seeing names. After hearing questions. After knowing the weight."

He nodded once, like a machine that still had one cog turning. "Yes."

"Then say it plain," I said. "Say you value your definition of order above their lives."

"I value the system," he said. "Without systems, there is chaos. Chaos costs more than the ledger can bear. I stood where others could not. I took the blame so others could sleep."

"You are asking us to honor your sacrifice," I said. "To bless the hurting because you called it prevention."

His one eye seemed to slip, as if some part of him wanted to look away and some other part could not. "History will justify me," he rasped. "Time will say I did what had to be done."

"History is written in the light of those who survive," I said. "Not in your comfortable rooms. Not on your glossy reports. History will not justify what children could not outrun."

He leaned back, the seams of his suit popping softly. The smell of rot seemed to thicken, pressing at the corners of the room. For a beat the basement felt like a courtroom and not the little cold place with a bulb and a tape recorder. I could feel the names. The boy with bread in his mouth. The sister with glass in her arms. Keisha on the pavement. Jordan's cap. The list went on, and the ghost tried to steady himself against it.

"What do you want me to do with you?" he asked finally.

"Nothing," I said. "You are already dead."

"No," he insisted. "I want to be remembered as necessary. I want a book that says I was brave. I want a plaque. I want my grandchildren to say I was a man who put the country first."

"You want your story cleaned," I said. "You want it scrubbed of the parts where you bled people for comfort."

He smiled, and it was a crack in porcelain. "Yes."

"You will get no plaque here," I said. "But you will get the truth. You will get names. You will get the faces you took. You will get the list of what was carried out of houses. You will get the baseball card. You will get the knitted cap. You will get the foil blanket and the torn eviction notice. You will get the Bible pieces. You will get the cardboard with the half sentence. You will get the phone and the patch. You will get the eyes that will not forgive you."

He closed his one milky eye as if the knowledge stung. "They will not forgive?" he asked.

"No," I said. "Not all of them. Some may find a way to breathe through what you did. Some may learn to live around it. But forgiveness is not your debt to demand. You cannot make amends with a policy memo. You cannot make apology with a press release. The people you broke will not hand you absolution."

He slumped, the dead weight of a man who had asked too much. The bulb above flared, then dimmed. For a long moment neither of us spoke. The recorder's red light blinked steady like a small heart.

"Do you regret?" I asked again.

His shoulders rose and fell once. "No," he said. "Not in the way you want. Regret is inefficient. It is a softness that breaks the machine. I do not believe in it."

"You do not," I said. "Then tell me this. When you signed, did you ever imagine you would be sat in a basement and asked to say the word 'sorry' directly to the people you destroyed?"

"No," he admitted. "I did not."

"Then maybe we should have given you less power," I said. "Power that needs no eyes is too dangerous."

He let out something like a sigh. "Perhaps."

"Perhaps will not undo the boy's breath," I said.

His mouth worked. He closed his hand into something like a fist, and for a second the room felt smaller, taut with the
112

sound of the living breathing around a dead man. "I bore it," he said again. "I bore it so others did not have to. If that makes me monster, then say so."

"I say you were both," I said. "You were a monster and a man who found ways to justify his comfort. You were capable of both."

He stared at the table, at his blackened nails, at the records of choices. He seemed very old suddenly, older than his death could legally allow, older than his suit.

"Will the world forgive me?" he asked faintly.

"No," I said. "Not for your deeds. Maybe for the hand you extended later. Maybe for the small things. But not for the buildings of cruelty you raised."

He leaned back. The chair scraped. The smell of rot thinned like a curtain lifting. "Then what do I get?" he breathed.

"You get what you cannot buy," I said. "You get the truth said aloud. You get the hymns that were silenced to be sung again. You get the names recited until they take up space in people's mouths. You get a small place among the witnesses."

He made a noise that might have been acceptance. Then, almost on a whim, he said, "Forgive me."

"Forgiveness is not yours to ask," I told him. "It belongs to those you hurt."

His milky eye blurred. He reached a hand out, and for an instant his fingers looked like the pens that signed away lives. Then, without ceremony, his shoulders sagged and his shape began to flake away, the suit collapsing like paper left in the rain. The room smelled of ash.

"You will not be the last," I said as his voice thinned. "There will always be men who think the ledger is more important than a mother's name."

"Perhaps," he whispered. "Perhaps."

The chair scraped back on its own. The milky eye dissolved. The suit slumped, an empty husk. The recorder kept blinking. The bulb swung gently. The basement was still again.

I leaned back, crossed my legs, and let the sugar smile stretch across my face.

"Next," I said.

~11
The Trial of Fire

The basement was hotter that night. The air clung to the skin, thick, almost oily. The bulb above buzzed louder than before, as though straining to hold its own against some unseen heat. I set the recorder on the table, pressed the red button, and felt the sweat bead on my neck.

"Oh gee," I said. "I am glad he is dead."

The door opened. Not one figure this time, but several. Shadows crowded the stairwell. Feet shuffled against concrete. One by one they filed into the room, the metal chairs clattering as though the building itself groaned under their return.

The boy with the singed hair sat first. His eyes were still blue, still haunted. He placed his scorched piece of door on the table.

Next came Rose, hood up, sleeves chewed, eyes dark. She laid down her folded drawing, lines sharp enough to cut.

The college student arrived with chains of torn paper, law books ripped at the spine. The poisoned woman set down her jar of cloudy water. The girl with the scars tugged her sleeves down tight, leaving drops of blood on the chair as she sat.

The mother with the cap. The protester with the cardboard scrap. Mateo with his foil. Danielle with her eviction notice. Luis with his prison patch.

They filled the room until no chair was left empty. The bulb swayed, its light flickering over their objects, their proofs. The heat grew thicker, as though the basement furnace had broken loose and filled the air.

I looked at them all. "Why are you here?"

The boy answered first, voice steady. "To repeat."

"Repeat what?"

"That I am glad he is dead," he said. His hand clenched the door fragment. "Because my mother and sister cannot speak, but I can. Because silence is the ground he wanted, and I will not give it."

Rose leaned forward. "I am glad he is dead," she said, her teeth bared. "Because his laughter will not echo again. Because no other girl will hear his voice and know it means ruin."

The college student spoke next, her eyes bright with fury. "I am glad he is dead. Because he cannot write chains anymore. Because my body is not a paragraph in his lawbook."

The poisoned woman lifted her jar, the water inside glinting sickly. "I am glad he is dead. Because he cannot sell my river for profit. Because my blood does not belong to his contracts."

The girl with the scars tugged her sleeves again. "I am glad he is dead. Because no more children will kneel in his office and call it prayer. Because the blade I hold now is mine, not his."

Lorraine pressed her son's cap flat on the table. Her voice broke but did not falter. "I am glad he is dead. Because no other mother should watch her child bleed on the street while men in uniform write notes."

Malik lifted the cardboard scrap. "I am glad he is dead. Because his baton is dust. Because silence no longer wears his name."

Mateo's foil crackled in his hands. "I am glad he is dead. Because no other child should sleep on stone and call it a bed. Because my mother's arms are stronger than his laws."

Danielle smoothed the eviction notice. "I am glad he is dead. Because families are not numbers. Because hunger is not a market. Because my daughter still has me, and that is more than he could take."

Luis dropped his patch on the table. "I am glad he is dead. Because I am not data. Because I am not profit. Because the machine stutters without his hand."

The bulb flickered. The heat pressed harder. Sweat slid down faces, down hands. The air shimmered.

"Do you all agree?" I asked.

"Yes," they said together, voices colliding, overlapping, shaking the walls.

"Does his death heal you?"

"No," they answered.

"Does his death restore the dead?"

"No."

"Then why glad?"

Their voices rose in waves.

"Because his silence cannot erase our names."

"Because he cannot touch another girl, another boy, another river, another home."

"Because the ground is stronger than his pen, his gun, his code."

"Because memory burns hotter than lies."

The objects on the table rattled. The bulb hissed, its filament glowing too bright, stretching toward breaking. The air was thick now, choking.

The boy with the blue eyes shouted, "He called my family acceptable losses. I call him unacceptable."

Rose shouted, "He thought power made him untouchable. Death touched him."

Lorraine shouted, "He said justice was a word. My son's blood was a sentence."

Luis shouted, "He said efficiency. I say cages. I say numbers. I say no."

The jar of poisoned water tipped and spilled across the table. The cardboard scrap soaked dark. The foil caught the light, flaring. The eviction notice curled at its edges. The cap absorbed water until it looked bloodied again.

The air roared like a furnace. The heat blistered the walls. The basement was fire, though no flames burned.

"Tell me," I said above the roar. "Who are you now?"

Voices rose, louder, overlapping until they were a chorus.

"I am the boy who lived."
"I am the girl who drew."
"I am the woman who tore laws apart."
"I am the river that still runs."
"I am the singer with scars."
"I am the mother who remembers."
"I am the protester who chants."
"I am the child who survived cages."
"I am the mother who endures."
"I am the man who will not be data."

Their words collided, a storm of declarations. The bulb burst, glass shattering, sparks spitting across the table. In the dark, the glow came from them, their objects shining with impossible heat, their faces lit from within.

I leaned forward, feeling the air burn against my skin. "And what do you demand?"

They answered as one. "That he stay dead. That he stay buried. That his memory be nailed to his deeds, not washed in excuses."

The fire inside them flared brighter, filling the basement with a light hotter than any bulb, brighter than any furnace. It roared through the silence, consuming the walls, the table, the air itself.

Still I sat, recorder blinking, catching every word.

And when the fire reached its peak, when the voices became unbearable, the light collapsed inward, leaving only darkness.

The objects remained on the table, steaming. The chairs stood empty. The basement was still.

I leaned back in the dark, crossed my legs, and let the sugar smile rise again.

"Next," I said.

~12
The Last Question

The basement was silent. The fire was gone, though the walls still seemed to tremble with its echo. The bulb above had burst, glass scattered across the floor. No light remained but the faint red blink of the recorder.

The chair opposite me sat empty. The objects still lay on the table, wet, burned, torn, scarred. Proofs of lives interrupted. Proofs of names.

For a long time I said nothing. My hands folded. My legs crossed. My breath slow. Then I leaned forward.

"And you," I said into the dark. "Who are you glad is dead?"

The recorder blinked. The silence stretched.

"Who?" I asked again, softer this time. "Who will you name, when the world tells you to forget? Who will you bury with your words, even if no one else listens?"

The basement waited. I smiled, sugar-sweet and sharp as a knife.

"This is where it ends," I said. "Or where it begins."

The recorder's light went dark.

About EATMS Productions

What's happening to women now is not random. It's structural.

Policy, culture, technology, and power are moving in the same direction.

EATMS maps them clearly and shows how to respond.

This title is part of an ongoing body of work. All EATMS Productions titles, across all series, authors, and formats, are components of a single connected project.

Start here: EATMS System Primer — Free Bundle
https://eatms.gumroad.com/l/dyvzbw

For full catalog or inquiries: eatms.me

Free survival booklet + EATMS updates: email "EATMS" to eatms@pm.me

Please feel free to burn part or all of this book, safely, as an effigy.